# Dr. Feelgood:

## *Carl Weber Presents*

Urban Books, LLC
97 N18th Street
Wyandanch, NY 11798

Dr. Feelgood: Carl Weber Presents
Copyright © 2016 Christian Keyes

ISBN 13: 978-1-62286-956-5
ISBN 10: 1-62286-956-7

First Trade Paperback Printing February 2016
Printed in the United States of America

10 9 8 7 6 5 4 3 2 1

*This is a work of fiction. Any references or similarities
to actual events, real people, living or dead, or to real
locales are intended to give the novel a sense of reality.
Any similarity in other names, characters, places, and
incidents is entirely coincidental.*

Distributed by Kensington Publishing Corp.
Submit orders to:
Customer Service
400 Hahn Road
Westminster, MD 21157-4627
Phone: 1-800-733-3000
Fax: 1-800-659-2436

# Dr. Feelgood:

## Carl Weber Presents

*Christian Keyes*

www.urbanbooks.net

# Dr. Feelgood:

## *Carl Weber Presents*

*Christian Keyes*

# Dedication

This book is dedicated to my son. Everything I do is for you, out of love for you, to provide for you. When I'm exhausted and don't feel like going anymore, my motivation is you. I also want to dedicate this to the loyal and consistent supporters, fans, friends, and family. After God, you all definitely help make this possible. #TeamKeyes

# Acknowledgments

I want to thank everyone who helped make this possible: God, Carl Weber, Martha Weber, N.D. Brown, Joylynn M. Ross and the whole Urban Books Media family. It's a huge blessing to be able to share my stories with the world, and you all have been instrumental and essential in making that happen. Thank you!

# Chapter 1

The sun peeked through the blinds and landed on Phil's broad shoulders. He sat at his desk in his office, deep in thought. It was 4:30, Friday afternoon. The city streets and expressways were lined with cars full of people rushing to get home. Traffic was barely moving on every major street, and any expressway was a parking lot. The L.A. skyline was still strong, busy, and beautiful, leading to 2600 Olive Street, the building that housed the offices of therapists Dr. Phillip Gooden and Dr. Marcus Collins.

Phil clenched the muscles in his jaw, and the tension showed through the low but groomed beard he was sporting. He focused his intense brown eyes on the small, cherry-wood box in his hand. It reflected the light as he raised it up to get a better look at it.

There was no turning back now, he thought. Shit just got real, and he knew it would get even more so once Denise finally arrived. She was always late, but he didn't mind. She usually made a grand, or at least memorable, entrance when she did finally show up; and somehow, no matter how irritated he was by her tardiness, one flash of her million-dollar smile and the world was great again.

Phil leaned back in his chocolate brown leather desk chair and glanced at the rose-gold Meister watch that hugged his right wrist. He was getting more nervous by the minute, knowing that she would be there shortly. He stood up and assessed his appearance. The tailored,

three-piece black DKNY suit he was wearing fit him like
a glove—not too tight, just right. He looked like a professional athlete, standing a chiseled six feet, three inches
tall and 200 pounds, with creamy peanut-butter skin.

Phil began to pace back and forth. "How will I ask?"
he wondered out loud. "What if she says no? Maybe
I shouldn't ask her today. Perhaps I should wait for a
better time."

He closed his eyes, took a deep breath, and shook off
the nerves. The knock on the door snapped him back to
reality. Showtime.

"Just a second," he said as he hurried to the desk to
hide the box in his drawer and sit down. Once he'd done
so, he put on the façade of a cool, calm, and collected
gentleman, knowing inside he was as nervous as a sinner
in church on Sunday. "Come on in."

The office door cracked open.

*Damn*, he thought as Denise sauntered into the room
with that "I know I'm late, but I'm beautiful, so it's okay"
look on her face. And it was okay.

"Good afternoon, Dr. Gooden," she said as she pulled
the door closed behind her.

Phil knew right away what she had in mind. She looked
at him like lunch, with those big, pretty brown eyes of
hers. A smile cascaded across her face as she slowly
started undressing.

Phil's nerves vanished as if they hadn't consumed him
just seconds ago. Denise had that effect on him, though.
She could make him forget all about his troubles—and
make him want to get into a little trouble with her.

"Lock the door," Phil said, and Denise did as she was
told. She always did. It was one of the many things that
Phil loved about her. She was such an accommodating
and enthusiastic lover. Phil couldn't remember a day
in the last several months that they hadn't made love,

and him getting head was a daily thing. Who said black women didn't go down? They surely weren't talking about Denise. She met all of Phil's desires and then some. Why would he not want this forever, especially considering the fact that he loved her immensely?

Phil looked up and saw that she had slipped off her shirt and skirt and was now standing in a candy-apple red Victoria's Secret set. He liked the way that red looked on her—so good against her pretty brown skin. Those yoga and spin classes had been paying off. Denise had always had a nice shape, but now she was putting most of those Instagram models to shame. She was thick, like Louisiana gumbo; her stomach was tight, those thighs were right, and that ass looked like the letter *P* from the side.

Phil couldn't wait any longer to get a taste of the supper before him that had his mouth watering. He began to undress. Jacket first, vest, then his shirt and tie. He thought for a second about whether he should get completely naked. After all, he was at work and it was business hours. Then he remembered that he was the boss and this was his therapy office, so he continued stripping down to the suit in which he was born.

He kicked off his Ferragamo dress shoes, stopped, and motioned for Denise to handle the rest, which she did gladly. Denise, Denise. This woman never had to be told something twice. Sometimes she didn't even have to be told once. She just knew. That was the connection she and Phil had. It went beyond just her being able to finish his sentences. She always seemed to know what he needed, when he needed it, and how much he needed. Most importantly, she knew when he needed nothing at all but to be left alone in his own thoughts. It was like this woman was a part of his soul. This had to be what people meant when referring to a soul mate.

Denise unbuckled his pants, took them down and off, then stopped to admire Phil, her own personal Dr. Feelgood. A pharaoh tattoo on his right arm, fraternity letters on the other, and a one-foot cross tattoo on the left side of his chest, with the bottom of it pointing down to his sculpted six-pack. Noticing the sizable imprint in his boxer briefs, she kissed his abs, one by one, as she slid his underwear to the floor, liberating her prize.

Phil gathered Denise's hair behind her head and held it for her. She preferred it that way. She paid way too much at her weekly hair appointments to get it all sticky and messy. That virgin Remy was expensive.

The warmth of her mouth comforted Phil's manhood. The flickering of her tongue teased the sensitive nerves at the tip of his mountain.

"Shit," Phil whispered as Denise tasted him, savoring the moment, standing there in his office, buck naked, free, proud, loved, feeling like an Egyptian king.

He noticed that even though she knew he was too long to fit it all in her mouth, she still tried. Never one to be selfish, Phil lifted Denise to her feet—by her hair—kissed her deeply, and took off her crimson bra. He kneeled down, pulled her panties to the side, and began to lick her honeypot while she was still standing. She almost lost her balance a couple of times, and her legs got weak, so he sat her on the desk and continued his intimate conversation with her candy land.

Sensing that she was ready to climax, he stood up, pulled her to the edge of the desk, wrapped her legs around his waist, and entered her. The way she inhaled sharply was music to his ears. He loved that shit.

She was the best lover he had ever had, hands down, but it had been mutually beneficial. Phil had given her the first of many multiple orgasms. He'd made her squirt for the first time, and he had taught her many other things about her body. This was *Fifty Shades,* and he was Phil Grey.

What started off as a soft moan from Denise, which was a sensual whisper to Phil's ears, rose to a higher pitch. This alerted Phil that not only was her voice climaxing, but her body was about to climax too. Phil made it his business to hit the spots in his lover's tunnel that would bring about the light at the end of the tunnel, so to speak.

Her arms tightened around him, and her thighs held him in place—in the place right where she needed him to be in order to get hers off. The two were like a well-designed sculpture one could display on the mantel of a bedroom corner fireplace. A work of art.

They came together in that same position. With a light sweat glistening on both their bodies, their breathing slowed, in sync. Without moving too much, Phil just looked at her for a moment, admiring his woman.

*She deserves it and she's worth it,* he thought.

Now was the time. He reached in his top desk drawer and grabbed the box. While still inside her, he opened the box up, revealing an immaculate three-carat, princess-cut diamond ring with a platinum band. The afternoon sun made it glow, and when Denise saw it, she froze, absolutely speechless. Her eyes darted from the ring to Phil's face. He saw surprise, joy, and love.

"Marry me?" Phil asked. As with a poet about to read a poem during open-mic night, if the poem had to be explained beforehand, then the poet hadn't done something right in relaying his or her thoughts. Phil didn't need to go into some long spiel about how he wanted to spend the rest of his life with Denise. If he'd been doing things right, then she already knew. He said all that needed to be said with every look, kiss, and gesture. The ring and the question that accompanied it were simply confirmation.

Although surprise, joy, and love still rested on Denise's face, there was something else there, only Phil wasn't sure exactly what it was. He could see her reaching for words, unsure of what to say.

Finally she spoke, all the while staring at the ring. "Yes," she said.

Phil hoped that it was just the shock of it all. He chose not to pay much attention to her apprehension, because he was elated that she had said yes. He put the ring on her finger and kissed her hand.

"I am so madly in love with you. You know that, right?" he said while looking into her eyes.

"I know," Denise said and smiled, taking her eyes off the ring to look into her fiancé's eyes.

The intercom beep startled them both.

"Dr. Gooden, Dr. Collins asked me to see if you still wanted to meet with him before your next appointment." The familiar sound of Julie's voice filled the office. She was Phil's office manager, slash assistant, slash secretary, slash everything.

Phil pressed the button on the phone and responded. "Thanks, Julie. You can send him over in five minutes."

Phil glanced around and noticed that he and Denise were both still naked. "Better make that ten."

"Will do."

Denise finished dressing before Phil. As he dressed, she sat silently, staring at the ring on her finger while holding the cherry-wood box that had housed the ring in her other hand.

Stealing gazes at Denise without her even noticing, Phil no longer felt all the anxiety he had been feeling earlier. The weight had been lifted, and the most important decision of his life had been made and carried out. He felt relieved as he finished dressing himself.

"All we need to do now is pick a date," he said as he kissed her forehead.

She smiled, but didn't say anything. After a moment, Denise looked at her watch, then to Phil. "I have to go, babe."

That was it? *I have to go, babe?* At least in movies the women took a couple minutes to gush over how much they loved the ring and/or the man who had blessed them with it. Phil was secure in himself and his love for Denise, so he opted not to concern himself with those thoughts as he brushed them aside.

"Well, I need to get back to work myself. I'll see you at home later?" Even though Denise had quite a few things at Phil's house—her own side of the closet, a vanity table and dresser—she still hadn't given up her condo in their two and a half years of dating. That was definitely something they would have to discuss, but not now, of course.

"Thanks for lunch," he said with a smirk as he hugged Denise. He didn't immediately release her from the embrace. Instead, he held her, hoping that the exciting energy he felt, knowing that soon he'd be married to the woman he loved more than anything in the world, would transfer to her. When he did finally pull back away from her, he looked her in the eyes and said, "I love you."

"I love you too," she replied then turned to leave. She stopped at the door and looked back at Phil.

He waited for her to say at least one line from the movies. "I can't wait to spend the rest of my life with you," or perhaps, "I've always dreamed of this day."

But she said nothing. She gave a soft smile, turned, and left, pulling the door slightly closed behind her.

Phil would have been a fool not to have noticed that Denise was acting a little out of character. He imagined this was all a shock to her, and this wasn't a movie. It was reality. So, he chalked her behavior up to the emotion surrounding the proposal. He was, after all, a psychologist, and the way she had acted could simply be explained by the pressure of the immense decision she had just made, coupled with the surprise of the proposal. Those two items combined with the powerful orgasm she'd just had made it was easy to see several logical possibilities for her reaction. Bottom line, she'd agreed to get married, and that was all that mattered. He smiled. He was happy; he was engaged. He was not going to allow his mind to drain fifty percent of the completely filled glass, leaving him to wonder and be torn over whether it was half full or half empty.

Phil straightened up his desk and wiped it down with a cloth. Then he sprayed some Febreze around the office, hoping to remove the pineapple-scented smell of sex in the air. Phil went into his private office bathroom and gave himself a quick wash-up. Afterward, he sat down at his desk and got back to work—or rather got to work. It was safe to say he really hadn't accomplished much that morning, anxious about his proposal to Denise.

Phil looked through the folder labeled *Dr. Marcus Collins*. It was his most recent assessment. He noted the subpar scores, lackluster performance, and the patient comments about him, none of which were good.

Right on cue, his colleague knocked on Phil's half open office door and walked in. Six feet two inches tall, dark-skinned, bald-headed and carefree, he looked like the brother that Morris Chestnut didn't know he had. Marcus's goatee was the only thing that was in order, though. His clothing definitely was not. He had on no tie or jacket, a stain on his untucked dress-shirt, and his pants looked like he had just taken a nap in them.

"Hey, Phil, you wanted to see me?"

"Yeah, grab a seat, Marc." Phil extended his hand to the chair on the opposite side of his desk.

Marc sat down in the chair. He looked like a student in the principal's office, as if he knew he had done something wrong but wasn't sure what he'd been caught doing.

"We have to talk about your latest evaluation," Phil started. "It wasn't wonderful . . . at all." Marc wasn't just a fellow therapist working for Phil. He was also Phil's best friend, which made it hard for Phil to tell Marc that his work ethic wasn't up to par. Separating business from personal was easier said than done.

"Oh, it's all good. It's just one review." There was Marc with his nonchalant attitude. Clearly he wasn't unable to separate business from personal either. They were obviously in the workplace discussing business matters, but Marc had just replied nonchalantly, like he was shooting the breeze with one of his homeboys.

"It's not just one review, Marc. Of the four you've had, three have been bad. This looks bad on you. And me. The board is on my back about your performance here, so we have to turn this around. They gave me the financial backing to start this practice because they trusted me. I can't have them thinking I'm showing you favoritism because you're my boy. My reputation to run an unbiased business is at stake here. Another one of these below standard reviews and they're going to push my hand at suspending you, maybe even firing you."

Marc shifted uncomfortably in his seat. "Can they do that?"

"Yes." Phil sighed and looked down at the review, shaking his head. "And I have to admit, it won't take much pushing on their part." He looked up at Marc, seeing the look of concern on his face, and feeling the sudden tension.

"We've been best friends for about ten years now," Phil said, "and I'm only telling you this because I don't want you to blow this opportunity. I know what you're capable of. That's why I went to bat for you with these guys to even get you in this office. They fought me tooth and nail because of your low GPA and lack of references." Phil nodded toward the papers before him. "And these reports have them looking at me like, *I told you so.*"

Marc exhaled. "I feel you. I can tighten things up."

"Thank you." Phil stood and crossed over to Marc and dapped him, to let him know that he still had his back. The tension in the room lifted.

"You've got to do better, bro," Phil said sincerely, but something inside him knew that it wouldn't be long before Marc went back to his wayward behavior.

Phil thought back over the years that he had known his best friend. Marc had always been that way: nonchalant and lackadaisical. That was partly why they got along so well. They were exact opposites and seemed to balance each other out. Phil had always been the responsible one, always striving for good grades. Marc, on the other hand, had always done just enough to get by.

Back in college, Marc had dropped a bunch of classes during his freshman and sophomore years. Because of that, he ended up a full year behind Phil, when he should have been graduating at the same time.

"This party will never die," had been Marc's mantra in the early years.

Phil could see that he was still living by that credo and if anything, it disappointed him. He had done all the groundwork, gotten the bank loans and investors to fund the therapy practice, found the building, renovated it, and even had a solid marketing campaign established in the city. He had pulled in dozens of court-ordered cases for things like mandatory anger management assessment and treatment, domestic violence offenders counseling, road rage therapy, and so on. The beauty of the state cases was that the city cut his practice a check directly for each patient, so they were basically printing money. Phil was clearing three hundred thousand dollars a year plus bonuses.

Then came Marc. He had graduated by the skin of his teeth; therefore, no self-respecting practice in the state of California would hire him. The only lead he had was as a county therapist, and the pay was $48,000 a year, before taxes. Marc couldn't even live paycheck to paycheck with that job. Phil knew, because Marc was always borrowing money from him.

Marc had tried to tough it out there for almost two years and had only recently quit. Phil had been sympathetic to Marc's hard luck story and went to the city medical board on his behalf. With Phil's reference, Marc was in. He had his own office, one hundred thousand a year to start, with the possibility of more when he picked up extra state cases. But, once again, Marc only did enough to get by, so there they were.

In the last couple of months, Phil often watched Marc come to work hung over from the night before. He had caught him multiple times "meditating naked" with the attractive female patients. Marc rarely wore a suit, which was plainly stated in the company dress code as a requirement. If he ever did wear one, it looked like he'd gotten it out of the dirty clothes basket.

Still, looking over at him, Phil could only see his potential. He knew that he couldn't give up on him, even with all his issues. He knew that he was basically the only family Marc had. Both of his parents had passed when he was young, and he had no brothers or sisters, which left only Phil.

Phil looked Marc dead in the eye, his look pleading with Marc for once in his life to be a man of his word.

"I got you. I'll handle it," Marc assured him as he stood.

"Okay, because this is it, the last warning. I got your back, but I'm not losing my job or my license for you."

Marc nodded in agreement and was fixing to leave before he thought of something. "Oh, by the way, did you do it?"

Phil looked puzzled.

"Did you propose to Denise?"

Phil threw his head back in remembrance. "Oh, yeah. I sure did." His face lit up.

"And I can tell by the look on your face that she must have said yes."

"Yep. I'm on my way to becoming a married man."

Marc began digging in his pocket. "Then hold on for a second." He pulled out his cell phone and took a picture of Phil.

"What did you do that for?"

"I needed a before picture."

"Before what?"

"Before you get married and she starts worrying you to death. You'll want a photo pre gray hair and beard."

"Oh, man, get out of here," Phil said, laughing.

Marc turned to leave. Phil watched him go. As the laughter died down, Phil hoped that this time, after being warned about his job performance, Marc would be different.

Phil noticed that he had a little time before his next appointment, so he logged into his MacBook and started searching for potential honeymoon destinations. He figured that, as with most women, Denise would want to handle all the particulars concerning the actual wedding, which he was fine with. Lord knows he didn't want to be picking out plates, cakes, and stationery.

With each island he clicked on, he envisioned what it would be like to have an elaborate and romantic getaway right after Denise became Mrs. Phillip Gooden. The mere thought brought a smile to his face and made his eyes light up.

*Yeah, she is the one I want to spend the rest of my life with,* he thought.

He bookmarked a few exotic locations, circled some possible dates on his calendar, and then shut down his computer. It was almost time for his session with his next patient.

There was a knock at the door.

"Come in," Phil called out.

The door opened, and in walked Julie Madison. Glowing mocha skin, pretty brown eyes, soup coolers parted, revealing that great smile of hers, she reminded Phil of Nia Long and Sanaa Lathan at the same time. Plus, she had the short Halle Berry cut and was always dressed to the nines. To top it all off, she was the consummate professional, always on the case when something needed to be done. Most times, she handled things before Phil ever had to ask her to.

When he had hired her three years earlier, there was an immediate and mutual attraction, but Phil didn't think it would be good to get involved with someone he worked with, so he never pursued her, and she offered him the same respect. Shortly thereafter, he and Denise became serious, and the rest was history.

The two coworkers were good friends, but neither Julie nor Phil ever crossed the line. It was sometimes difficult for him to watch her with other guys, not because he was attracted to her, but because she had the worst luck picking men. She always seemed to choose the wayward ones, or the most unfaithful. This bothered Phil, because he could see that she was truly a good woman who deserved better, but other than reminding her of that fact occasionally, he just stayed in his lane.

"Hey, Julie, what's going on?" Phil asked.

"You got a minute?" she asked. Her tone was nondescript.

"Sure. Grab a seat if you want."

"It'll be quick." She paused for a second.

"There's a strange but pleasant smell in here. What is that?" she asked, knowing good and damn well what it was. Everyone could detect the scent of sex in the air.

"Uhh, I don't smell anything," Phil said, almost convincingly. He then quickly shifted the focus back to her. He clasped his hands together, elbows on his desk. "So what did you need?"

"Oh, I don't want to get anyone in trouble, but can you please ask Dr. Collins to ease up on the flirting? He gets a little carried away, not to the point of harassment, but it's a bit too much sometimes."

Julie's complaint, unfortunately, did not surprise Phil. The only thing that surprised him was that Julie hadn't been in his office to complain about it sooner. Phil had never witnessed Marc flirting with Julie. He thought Marc would have at least shown him the respect of not jeopardizing the working relationship with his office manager. Leave it to Marc to yet again disappoint his friend.

"I will mention that to him," Phil said, "but I didn't hear it from you." He smiled, letting Julie know that she didn't have to worry about Marc coming at her funny for blowing the whistle on him.

"Thank you. He's a nice guy, just not really my type," she replied with a smile of her own.

"Anything else I can help you with?"

Phil could tell that she wanted to say something; her eyes gave it away. He knew that she probably wasn't getting her womanly needs met, but it wasn't his place to speculate.

She damn near bit her lip off trying not to state her real answer—the one that involved releasing years of attraction and sexual tension. The response that would declare that she was strong and passionate, but for Phil, she would be submissive, let him take control and sexually dominate her.

The fact that she had picked up on the smell of good lovin' in the air and even mentioned it, just to let him know that she knew, said a lot. But alas, Phil was a committed man who was happily in love with the woman of his dreams, so even knowing all these things, he stayed professional and faithful. He prided himself on his self-control as he let the moment between them pass.

The ring of the phone coming from Julie's desk right outside of Phil's door in the lobby returned the room to its normal climate.

"Guess I better get that," she said as she left the office in a backpedaling motion.

"Saved by the bell," Phil said to himself as he heard her answer the call. Then he whispered in God's direction, "You didn't say there wouldn't be temptation, just that you would always provide a way out. Thanks, big guy."

# Chapter 2

Phil had a knack for knowing when someone wanted to say something and wasn't doing so. As he looked at his patient, Mr. Hartfield, he knew this was the case. Mr. Hartfield was your typical Caucasian male. At thirty-seven years old, he worked in corporate America, was good at his job, and made good money. He had been married for twelve years, but apparently there were some things wrong about the relationship that he didn't know how to disclose or deal with.

"This is the thing, Doc," he said then paused again. Hesitation rested in not only his tone, but his eyes.

"There is no judgment in this room, Mr. Hartfield," Phil said. "Just close your eyes and say it."

He closed his eyes, inhaled deeply, and blurted out, "My wife doesn't give me special attention anymore." Then he exhaled, as if he had been dying to get that off his chest.

From past experience, Phil was aware that there was more that would pour out: more problems, issues, and fears. "Continue," Phil said in a calm voice, preparing for the tidal wave of emotions from his client.

"She just doesn't seem to take an interest in doing it. At all! And I am always more than willing to do my part. She literally has to tell me to stop; that's how attentive and selfless I am when it comes to her. If I'm being honest, I can't remember the last time she took care of me that way."

Phil sat there in thought for a second. He wanted to make sure Mr. Hartfield was opening up the door for him to walk through. People came to therapists for many reasons, but to have a safe place to emotionally unload was one of the main reasons. Listening was an art form, and Phil made it a point to know when to do so and when to speak.

The questioning desperation in his client's stare let him know that he was now ready for his input.

"See, first of all," Phil said, "I've never liked the term *special attention*. That is something that should come naturally and regularly in any healthy marriage, from both sides." No, Phil had never been married himself, but he'd studied this kind of thing. He'd been trained on how to treat patients dealing with this issue and many other problems. Not only had he been trained through books and lectures, but through real life experiences via other clients who had found themselves in similar circumstances. Whether they knew it or not, they had taught him a thing or two.

"Was it taking place consistently before you two got married and right after the wedding?" Phil asked.

"Yes, all the time. Three or four times a week. And now, nada." Mr. Hartfield slumped in his chair, looking dejected.

Phil knew that he not only had to give him some help, but some hope as well. "I won't lie; that's a tough one, Mr. Hartfield."

"You're telling me. I'm faithful! And I love my wife, but any good marriage is built on love, trust, and *special attention*!" Never mind the fact that Phil didn't like using the label "special attention." That's what he wanted from his wife, and by golly he was going to call it how he saw it—or felt it. Or perhaps didn't feel it.

"I agree, but there are a few components that you left out, like communication, friendship, passion, appreciation, and more. Wouldn't you agree?"

Mr. Hartfield nodded in agreement.

"Good, then we're on the same page. There's something I want you to do when you get home today. Now, you get there before your wife, correct?"

"Yes." Mr. Hartfield sat in anticipation of whatever it was the good doctor could suggest to help turn his marriage around in the "special attention" department.

"Okay. I need you to follow my instructions to the letter." Phil handed him a piece of paper and a pen.

Mr. Hartfield positioned himself to begin taking notes.

"When you get to your house, shave your facial hair into the style she compliments you on the most. Next, take a shower, a real one, not a 'ho bath.'"

Mr. Hartfield attentively wrote down everything Phil said.

"Put on the pair of jeans that your wife likes to see you in. You probably know the ones I'm talking about, the ones that she compliments you on the most. Socks, with no holes, and a wife-beater. Not an old, faded gray one that's brown under the arms. A white one. Splash on just a little of the last bottle of cologne that she bought you."

Mr. Hartfield looked up with the first sign of disagreement since Phil had begun giving him instructions. "Doc, I hate that one though. It smells like the Garden of Eden."

"So what?"

"What do you mean, so what? I'm a man. Men aren't supposed to smell like gardens and flowers and stuff."

"She didn't buy it for you," Phil reasoned. "She got it because the idea of you wearing it turns her on, and it shows that you appreciate all the time she spent picking it out."

Mr. Hartfield took in Phil's words then looked back down at his writing material. "Cologne, Garden of Eden," he whispered as he jotted down more notes.

"Now, when you hear her pulling into the garage, I want you to start vacuuming the living room."

Mr. Hartfield snapped his neck up. "What? First you want me to walk around wearing that fragrance that I can't even pronounce, and now I have to do housework?" Disgust was an understatement for how he felt about Phil's latest suggestion. With furrowed brows, it was clear that he was starting to wonder if it was worth what he was paying an hour for this type of advice.

"In an average day, your wife sees you about forty times, if you count each time you enter and leave the room," Phil said. "After twelve years of marriage, she has seen you more than a hundred and fifty thousand times. At that point, and after twelve years of marriage, one of the sexiest things she will ever see you do is chores. Trust me. If you do what I'm suggesting, I guarantee that you will get a healthy dose of *special attention*."

Mr. Hartfield let out a gust of wind. He gave his note-pad his attention once again. "If you say so, Doc." He shook his head the entire time while writing. "If you say so."

"I know so," Phil said with certainty. "So do you think you can do that?" Phil waited for confirmation from his somewhat rebellious patient.

Mr. Hartfield shrugged. "I suppose I can do that for you, Doc."

"You're not doing it for me. You're doing it for your-self," Phil corrected. "And more importantly, you're doing it for your wife. And it doesn't have to stop there," Phil continued. "If your wife is doing the dishes, grab a towel, help dry and put them away. Or, after dinner, DVR the program you want to see, hand her the remote, and tell her to go relax and watch TV. You clean the kitchen once in a while. It's the ultimate aphrodisiac for women." Phil could see that Mr. Hartfield was still somewhat skeptical.

"How do you know this chore-head thing is going to work?"

A sincere and satisfied smile eased across Phil's face. "Let's just say, I do a *lot* of chores."

Mr. Hartfield jumped up out of his seat and headed for the door, startling Phil.

"What's the rush?" Phil looked down at his watch. "Your time's not up."

"I gotta go! I need to stop on the way home and grab some new socks and a pack of wife-beaters. All mine are gray with the brown under here." He pointed to his armpit. He was out of the room before he finished talking.

"Let me know how it goes," Phil said, calling after him.

"I will. Thanks, Doc!"

Phil sat there laughing for a moment. He felt good, like he was actually making a difference. He had heard people say, "One person can't change the world." He didn't buy that. He believed that if he could help make one person's life or marriage better, then he'd just made their world better.

Phil popped open his leather briefcase and placed his laptop and a few file folders inside. He closed it, looked around his office so as not to forget anything, then walked out. He hummed "Matrimony" by Usher and Wale, as he thought about what good food and great lovin' he would enjoy with his new fiancée all weekend long.

Marc and Julie were at her desk discussing Marc's appointment calendar when Phil walked up.

"I'm out of here. I hope you guys have a great weekend," Phil said.

"Already?" Julie asked.

"That was my last appointment for the day, and if I leave now, by the time Denise makes it to my place, I'll be naked with my work boots on," he said with a laugh, but he still caught the look Julie shot him over his last remark. Perhaps there was a little envy that she didn't have anyone at her house waiting for her with work boots on.

"I've got some work boots too, Julie. Brand new, crispy pair of Timberlands. You got plans this weekend?" Marc said proudly.

"No, thank you. I met someone, and if all goes well, I'll be curled up with him all weekend." Julie wriggled in her seat.

She had put a little something extra on her statement, but Phil intentionally opted not to catch it.

"I'm in the wind," Phil said, waving good-bye as he walked off. "See you guys Monday." He stopped and turned around. "Oh, yeah, Marc, if you go play ball Saturday, hit me up."

"Will do," Marc said without taking his eyes off Julie.

As Phil exited the lobby, he could hear Marc still flirting with Julie as he walked outside. He'd have to have that conversation with Marc about his flirting habits soon, but right now, it would have to wait.

He hopped in his chocolate, 4-door Porsche Panamera. It had the dark brown leather and wood-grain interior to match. He sat inside, motionless for a moment, as he did every day after work, just so he could turn his mind off from work and enjoy the drive home. A couple calming breaths and he pulled off.

Traffic was the same as usual in L.A.—bad. He didn't care, though. He was singing along to the song on the radio, "Together We Are Love," by Christian Keyes, and thinking about Denise.

Out of nowhere, and without signaling, a silver BMW changed lanes right in front of him, almost running him off the road. Phil didn't love this at all, but with all the counseling he did for people with anger issues and road rage, he had to keep his cool.

Phil pulled up next to the offending car at the next red light, rolled down the window, honked, and motioned for the other driver to roll down his. The guy obliged. He was a typical L.A. driver: young, image-conscious guy wearing Ray-Ban shades and texting while driving.

"Nice car, man. Is that new?" Phil asked.

"Yes, thank you," he said proudly, tapping on the steering wheel as if petting his dog.

"Fully loaded?"

"Yep, got all the options," the man proudly responded.

"That's great. Maybe next time you can use your damn blinker when you change lanes! You almost ran me off the road! What the hell is wrong with you?" Phil yelled.

Phil startled the guy so badly that he took off and made a quick right. Phil laughed, rolled up his window, turned his music back on, and continued driving.

On the way home, he made a quick stop at one of several floral shops he frequented to pick up a nice arrangement for his baby. He rarely bought her red roses. That was too easy, in his opinion. Anybody could stop at a grocery store and buy those.

Instead, he learned her favorite three colors: coral, lavender, and white. He would get her different types of flowers in those hues. From orchids to carnations, lilies to jasmine, gardenias to alstroemeria, Phil got her assorted and amazing bouquets every week. Phil liked that it took effort to research and find the flowers for Denise. He even knew what each kind stood for. He was damn near a florist at this point, with all he had learned, but in his mind, she was definitely worth it.

Phil was at the counter, waiting to check out with two dozen coral-colored roses. Apparently the woman in front of him and the woman behind him were friends, because he could see the looks they were giving each other. Little did they know that he was big on non-verbal communication. He also was always very aware of his surroundings and never missed much, so he saw the woman behind him pretending to grab his ass in the reflection in the window.

"Do you want to jump up here with your friend? I don't mind," Phil asked the woman behind him with a smile. The question caught her off guard.

"Ummm. Yes, please," she said as she gathered her things and went to stand with her friend. The whispering and giggling gave away most of their conversation. Phil saw them look at the flowers he was buying.

"Lucky woman," one of the women said and smiled.

"Nah, I'm the lucky one," he said, returning her smile.

After the two friends had paid for their purchases, one of them turned to Phil and slid her business card into his inside jacket pocket.

"In case you ever stop feeling so lucky," she said with teasing lips.

The cashier had a front row seat to this whole scene and found it to be hilarious. Phil politely smiled at the two very attractive ladies as they walked away.

"Have a nice day," he said to them.

Once they were out of sight, he took the woman's business card out of his jacket pocket and set it on the counter. He paid for what he came for and left without a word. He was used to this type of behavior from women. It wasn't the first time, and it wouldn't be the last. He was flattered, but it never went to his head. In his mind, he was just a nice-looking guy with a good job, making great money, and he had his stuff together. But he understood that was rare, especially for him to be only thirty-two years old. It meant that he was old enough to know what he was doing, but still young enough to get the job done, whatever it was.

Back in his car, he inhaled the beautiful scent of the flowers. He couldn't help but chuckle, thinking that would be the scent Mr. Hartfield would soon be donning. According to him, the cologne his wife had bought him smelled a lot like the bouquet he had just bought. Phil placed the flowers in the passenger seat of the car, pulled the door closed, and hesitated for a second. He realized that he was only a few miles from his parents' home.

It had been a few weeks since he had been by, so he figured he would pay them a quick visit. The last time he had been over there, they were having a bit of trouble, so what better time to check on them? He looked at his watch, calculating that he still had plenty of time to beat Denise to his place, so he started the car and headed to see his folks.

Upon arriving at his parents' home, Phil stood in the front yard for a while, just reminiscing, thinking back to his childhood. This was the same house he had grown up in. Yeah, it had been remodeled some. He had paid for the most recent series of upgrades as an anniversary gift to them, but it still felt like home. It even still smelled like it. That L.A. wind would push past his shoulder, carrying with it the sweet scent of bread from the bakery about a block away. That had always made him hungry as a kid, and it still had the same effect on him now.

He missed the good old days but looked forward to future days. Perhaps in years to come, his very own son might stand outside of his and Denise's home, experiencing this very same kind of moment. Phil smiled, took one more glance around, then went inside the door that he knew always stayed unlocked in the daytime.

"Pop, it's me. Don't shoot," Phil said with a chuckle as he knocked on the door and walked in. He was still partially serious though. About a year ago, Phil had come by one evening to check on the house, because he thought his parents were gone for the weekend. Turned out that they'd had a big fight, and only his mother had left. His dad, Clifton Gooden, had stayed there drinking his sorrows away. When Phil keyed his way into the house, his father thought he was a burglar and pulled a shotgun on him. Ever since then—day or night—Phil always announced, loud and clear, that it was him entering the home, to avoid any confusion.

"Come on in, son," Clifton said as he walked into the living room.

Phil took a good look at his dad. The man still had it. He was often mistaken for Billy Dee Williams, because he looked just like him. He was wearing a white V-neck T-shirt that read *Black Don't Crack* on the front. It was nothing but the truth, because Clifton was fifty-five years old, looking closer to forty than sixty.

Phil crossed over to his father and gave him a big hug. "How are you, Pop?"

"Good, son. No complaints. It doesn't help anyway." Clifton let out his usual deep, hearty laugh.

Phil walked back to the kitchen and looked inside. At this time of day, that was usually where he would find his mother, preparing dinner. "Where's Mom?"

There was no verbal answer from Clifton, so Phil walked back over to him.

"Where's Mom at?" Phil repeated, standing directly in front of his dad, waiting on an answer.

Again no response, but Cliff's melancholy face said it all.

"You guys have another fight?" Phil said, sounding exasperated. His parents were too old to still be having these catty fights.

"Yeah." Mr. Hartfield sounded just as exasperated as his son.

Phil knew it was time to sit down. This wasn't going to be the quick pop-in visit he'd originally thought it would be. He hated seeing his father like this, so he sure couldn't leave him this way, no more than he'd allow one of his patients to leave his office any worse off than they had been before they came.

"How long has she been gone?" Phil inquired.

"Just since around noon. She'll be back later. She's never gone for more than a few hours."

The look on his father's face, the look of just being tired, his heart being tired and brokenhearted, chipped away a piece of Phil's heart as well. He got up and went and sat down next to his dad. This wasn't some patient he had to sit across the room from and analyze; this was his father.

With that thought, Phil had to tread lightly. His father needed a listening ear, a sounding board. Phil didn't want to come off as if he were pointing fingers or placing the blame on him. That would have been the quickest way to make him shut down. He definitely didn't want to cause any strain on their father-son relationship either. It had always been good, and that was the way he wanted to keep it.

"What happened this time?" Phil asked apprehensively and without blame.

His father raised his hands in wonderment. "Who knows?"

"Well, if anybody should, it's you."

Clifton just sat there in his favorite recliner, shrugged his shoulders, and shook his head. He spoke no words.

"Pop, you know you can talk to me, right?"

"Yeah."

"So, what's going on? It seems like once a month you two have some huge argument and one of you has to leave the house to cool down. Is it infidelity?"

"No." Clifton shook his head adamantly.

"Are you sure?"

"Yes. She's not messing around, and I'm damn sure not. Hell, I haven't had any in months. That's part of the reason we argue."

Phil could see that his father was no longer wearing his poker face. It was clear in his eyes and in his voice that this was really bothering him, and that it had the potential to damage their marriage more than it already had.

"How long has it been like this?" Phil probed.

"A year or so."

"Have you talked to her about it?"

"Yes! Plenty of times!"

"I know you, Dad. Did you calmly talk to her about it, or did you get frustrated and start fussing like you do sometimes?"

"A little of both."

"That's part of the problem right there."

"Well, the other part must be them damn pills. I'm pretty sure her doctor put her on some new medication right around the time we started having troubles. It was supposed to help her, but nothing's changed." He took in a deep breath and exhaled pure frustration. "Only gotten worse, if you ask me."

Phil was surprised to hear that his mother had been prescribed some type of medication. If anything medical was going on with her, she usually never hesitated to talk to Phil about it. "Do you know what it's for?"

"Nope. She didn't want to talk about it. They're proba-bly up in her bathroom, in her medicine cabinet."

Curiosity had already gotten the best of Phil five seconds ago, when his father first mentioned the pills. "I'll be right back," Phil said as he moved quickly up the stairs, taking two at a time. He was only up there for a couple minutes then came right back down.

"I think I know what it is," Phil said as he walked back over to where his father was sitting.

Clifton perked up slightly, with a hopeful look on his face.

"Her new medications are for the treatment of the symptoms of menopause."

"Okay, but what does that have to do with the way she's been acting?"

Phil sat down again. "Everything. When women go through menopause, they can get depressed. Their hormones fluctuate and get off track. Sex can become painful for them, or they may lose the urge to have it all together. Often, women feel like less of a woman when they experience this, and that's probably why she didn't talk to you about it, or me. It's almost like the female equivalent of impotency." Phil really did sound like a doctor talking to a patient, but he had to be thorough in explaining the situation to his father. He didn't want him to take his mother's actions personally.

"Wow, I had no idea. So how do we help her fix this?"

"I got her doctor's name from the pill bottle. I'm going to look him up and call him in the morning. I'm going to try to have him change her medication, but that's only the beginning. This is going to take a little time, Pop, so you're going to have to be patient with her, communicate with her. That's your wife and the love of your life. Don't just tell her, but show her that she is still all woman to you. Run her a bath, give her a massage, cook her dinner. Put up a fight for what you love. You taught me that."

Clifton looked Phil in the eye and thought for a second. "I did always tell you that, and here you are, giving my advice back to me," he said with a smile. "All right, son. I can handle that. I'll do whatever it takes."

"That's what I want to hear." Phil raised his hand for his father to shake in agreement, which he did.

Clifton relaxed back on the couch, glad to have gotten to the bottom of things. It was a weight off his shoulders, knowing that there was hope for him and his wife's marriage. "Well, Dr. Feelgood, what's going on with your situation?"

"Situation?" Phil asked, confused. The last time he checked, he and Denise were more than okay in the sex department. Menopause wasn't anywhere near invading their sexual relationship. "My fiancée and I are just fine, thank you very much," Phil said proudly, trying not to cheese too much.

"Your what?" Clifton jumped to his feet. "You really did it." The last time the men had talked, the tables were turned, and it was Clifton giving his son advice. Phil had mentioned to his father that he felt Denise was the one. Clifton's advice was, "Put a ring on it then." The two had laughed about the response, but that's exactly what Phil ended up doing.

"Yes, sir!" Phil smiled. "I did it. I asked Denise to be my wife." He looked in his father's eyes. "She's the one, Pop."

"Are you sure?" his father asked.

"Absolutely!" Phil had complete certainty in his tone, in his expression. His lips weren't saying anything different than his eyes were speaking.

"How do you know?"

Phil thought about his answer briefly. "Because I would fight for her and love her through anything she ever had to deal with." He put his hand on his father's shoulder. "Just like you are willing to do with Mom." He winked at his father.

"Good answer, son," Clifton said with a proud smile.

"I had a good teacher," Phil said, smiling back.

Clifton and Phil gave one another a hearty hug.

"I'm happy for you," Clifton said, patting Phil on the back as he released him from the hug.

"Thanks, Dad." Phil stuck his hands in his pockets and looked down at the floor, almost like a bashful schoolboy who'd just told his favorite girl that he liked her.

"So, gimme the details." Clifton sat back down on the couch. "When'd you ask her, and how'd you pop the big question?"

"I asked her today, actually, but I can't really go into how I did it. There weren't a lot of clothes involved, if you know what I mean," he said with a smirk, still standing.

"I should've known. My son is a freak." Clifton shook his head, knowing his son all too well. Prior to this menopause thing, Clifton was a regular Casanova himself.

"Hey, I learned it from you," Phil said as they shared a much-needed laugh. "Speaking of Denise, I better go. I want to get home before her."

"More naked shenanigans?" Clifton raised an eyebrow.

"Yes, sir."

Again, they laughed together. Phil liked seeing his father happy, and he knew that they both had some work to do if they were going to put a smile back on his mother's face, but at least now they had a plan.

"Remember, have patience with Mom," Phil told his father sincerely as he prepared to leave.

"I got you." He shooed his hand at his son. "You don't have to tell me twice. I'm not hardheaded like you were coming up."

The corners of Phil's mouth turned up. "All right then, Pop. I'm out." Phil leaned down and hugged his father before heading for the door. "I love you. And tell Mom I stopped by and that I love her too," Phil called out before he left the house, got in his car, and headed home.

It had been an eventful day to say the least, but that was how every day of Phil's life played out. Different day, different client, different issues to resolve, but he would, just like all the other days, check that in at the door. One thing Phil never did was bring work home. One thing was for certain: he did put in work while he was at home. As he drove, he thought, with a devilish grin, *Now, where are my work boots?*

# Chapter 3

Phil drove slowly through his neighborhood. There were a lot of young children that lived on his street, and the last thing he ever wanted to do was hit one of them. When he'd picked out his home, it didn't go unnoticed by Phil that the neighborhood was more family oriented, not the typical area where a young, handsome bachelor would want to drop anchor. Deep inside, Phil must have known that eventually he would fit right in with his neighbors. First came love, next came marriage. If he had his way, in a couple of years, Denise would be pushing a baby carriage. Maybe two.

He was finally where he wanted to be in life. He had the woman of his dreams, a career that paid very well, and a dream home. Phil's real estate agent, Kendra Michelle, had actually been a patient he had helped through a rocky period in her marriage. With Phil's help, she eventually ended up saving and revitalizing it. So, as a thank you to him, she worked some real estate magic and got him into this million-dollar home, in a very nice neighborhood, for 600K. How she did that was beyond him, but he was grateful. He knew doctor jargon, but real estate language was foreign to him. All he recalled was something about some points here, some points there, a discount for this, and a discount for that, then voila! He had the keys to the most beautiful home he'd ever seen. Not to mention that he was one of only three African American homeowners on the street. The other two homes were owned by a lawyer and a CEO of some huge corporation.

As he pulled up, the sun was setting right behind the roof of his enormous five-bedroom, five-bathroom, two-story house, complete with a three-car garage, swimming pool, and hot tub in the back. Who wouldn't want to live in a luxurious and enormous place like this? He had opted for extra bedrooms because eventually, even though settling down wasn't something the average successful man in his thirties who could have any woman he wanted had on his mind, Phil always knew that one day he wanted to get married and have some kids to fill those rooms. He had grown up with no siblings and wanted at least two or three little ones of his own.

The idea of this made him light up every time the thought crossed his mind. Even though he definitely still had to discuss his and Denise's final living arrangements once they were man and wife, he couldn't imagine she'd want them to live in her condo versus his big ol' home. Besides, it wasn't like she didn't spend the majority of the time there anyway, and whenever they referred to "home," it was clear they meant the house . . . his house . . . soon to be *their* home.

Phil grabbed his things, got out of his car, and just stood there looking around. The same way he'd taken a minute to stare at his parents' home and think about his childhood, he thought about what it was going to be like for his children to grow up in this house; to play tag in this yard. The sound of the neighbor's lawn mower brought him back to the moment. Phil checked the mailbox. He flipped through the couple pieces of junk mail and then went inside.

He closed the door behind him and disarmed the alarm system, set his briefcase by the door like he always did, then laid his jacket on the armrest of the sofa. The house felt cold to him, but he paid it no mind. Believe it or not, he'd turned on his fireplace quite a few times throughout the year. Those who never lived in California thought that it was always sunny and hot. There was quite the evening chill.

Phil took the flowers into the kitchen and cut a half inch off of each stem, then grabbed a vase and filled it halfway with water. He put them inside and adjusted the flowers so they looked more presentable. He placed them on the table in the center of the living room. Mission accomplished. Denise was going to love them.

He had the number to Philippe Chow saved in his iPhone, because it was a favorite dining spot for both of them. He called and made reservations for 9 p.m. Surely Denise would want to celebrate their engagement over dinner.

Nine o'clock might have seemed late to have dinner, but he planned on manhandling her as soon as she walked in the door. After that, they both would need a little time to shower and get dressed, as well as being in need of nourishment. A late reservation should allow them plenty of time.

Phil looked around. Besides the slight chill in the room, something still felt different, but he wasn't sure what it was. What he did know was that he needed to find those work boots before Denise got there. He wanted to be waiting right by the front door for her, butt naked, with Timberlands on and two glasses of champagne. He was planning to pop the cork as she pulled in the driveway. He was pretty sure his Tims were upstairs in his closet, so he headed up to get them.

Phil began humming "The Hills" by the Weeknd. It just randomly popped into his head. He made a mental note to remember to have that playing when Denise walked inside as well. The song was aggressive, passionate, powerful, and you could make love to it, have sex to it, and fuck to it—and Phil and Denise did all three on the daily.

Arriving in his bedroom, he made his way over to the closet. Pressed for time, he went straight to his side, where he'd last placed the boots. He bent down and grabbed his boots but didn't rise back up. He was stuck, still, frozen stiff. He had to think for a moment. Had his eyes just deceived him?

He turned and looked to the left of the closet, which was Denise's side. He slowly rose into an upright position, dropping the boots. Swallowing hard, he took a step. It was like his feet were stuck in cement, but somehow he managed to take another step, and then another, until he was flicking at the hangers that just this morning had held Denise's clothing. Now the hangers were empty. There was no sign that Denise had ever been there. Phil looked down on the floor. There were a couple of hangers on the ground, but not a shoe, not a scarf. . . . Nothing.

He walked out of the closet and then headed over to Denise's vanity. There were a couple of forgotten safety pins, bobby pins, and an earring back or two, but her favorite fragrances—gone. The makeup that Phil had told her on more than one occasion that she didn't need due to her natural beauty—gone. Not even any leftover nail polish.

Next, Phil made his way over to his dresser, where he'd been kind enough to give her the top two drawers. They were empty. He closed his eyes and tried to think for a minute. His mind was blank, though. Not one reason came to mind why Denise's things were gone. He would have loved to conclude that the home had been robbed, but who breaks in just to steal some feminine items? Then there was the farfetched idea that maybe Denise decided to take her clothing to the drycleaners—all her clothing—but that wouldn't explain her personal items.

"Personal items," Phil said under his breath then quickly moved into the master bathroom. "Damn," he said upon seeing that Denise's toothbrush and toiletries were even gone. "What the hell?"

Finally a cohesive thought did enter his mind, but he still didn't want to face it. "Ah-ha!" he said, darting down the steps to the kitchen. He nearly broke his neck trying to get to the bottom landing, but once he got there, he headed straight for the kitchen. He walked over to the cupboard to the left of the stove and flung open the door. Any expression of hope he had on his face dissolved to nothing. The mug she drank her tea out of in the morning was gone. It was part of the matching set of her great grandmother's good china.

"She's gone," Phil said, finally having to admit the inevitable.

He walked back into the living room in what felt like slow motion to him. Yes, he'd found his boots exactly where he thought they were, but what he'd also found was that there wasn't even a remnant of Denise in the home. It didn't add up. There had not been a single trace of her or her belongings anywhere in the house.

Now, with a growing sense of urgency, he hurried throughout the main floor, still searching for anything of hers, but every trace was gone. He didn't understand. Phil walked over to the couch and flopped down. He pulled out his cell phone, and for the next twenty minutes, he called and texted Denise repeatedly, with no answer and no response.

Realizing his attempts to contact her were in vain, he went back on a search through the house for even just the slightest clue as to what was going on. He kept searching around the house until he got to the dining room, the only place that he hadn't checked. He froze as he took his first step inside it.

There it was, sitting in the center of the dining room table: that same cherry-wood box he had given her with the ring when he had proposed earlier that day. Phil walked over to the box and picked it up, then set it back down, afraid of the answers to unasked questions that he may find inside.

There was a handwritten letter on the table as well. This couldn't be good. Phil felt the strength leaving his legs, but he fought the urge to sit down. He needed a minute to mentally prepare himself for the letters that made up the words, that made up the sentences, that made up the paragraphs. He grabbed the top of one of the chairs to steady himself, reached for the box, and flipped it open. Sure enough, staring him in the face was the same three-carat, princess-cut diamond ring he had designed himself for Denise. That was no surprise. Somewhere inside, he had already known the ring would be in the box. It was just a tactic to delay doing what he really needed to do.

He picked up the letter in the other hand and read it.

*My dearest Phil,*

*I am so sorry for leaving like this, but it was the only way. I knew if I tried while you were home that you would talk me into staying. You are an amazing man, and any woman would be blessed to call you her own. You're going to make some woman the luckiest girl in the world someday . . . just not me. I love you, Phil, but I am not ready to get married.*

*I love what we had. It was fun, passionate, spon-taneous, and incredible on every level. But that's all I can handle right now. I want to travel, have fun, live, and be free to do as I please right now, and the finality of your proposal today scared the hell out of me. I know us moving in together was going to come up soon as well. Guess I'm not as ready as*

*I thought I was, and I know it will only hurt you worse if I leave later.*

*P.S. The ring is the one I always dreamed of having, but I think you should keep it. And please, don't come after me. My mind is made up. If you love me, you'll let me go.*

*Love Always,*
*Denise*

Phil had done a great job of being strong while reading the letter. His eyes had filled with tears, but not one had fallen. He glanced over at the ring again and that was it; the dam broke. The first one, then a second, and a third. Then there were too many tears to count. He let go of the note, and it sailed slowly back and forth until it landed on the floor. He closed the box and then walked, as if in a trance, into the kitchen.

He grabbed the bottle of Ace of Spades champagne he'd had chilling in the refrigerator since that morning, in hopes that Denise would say yes to his proposal. With the bottle in hand, Phil headed for the sliding doors that led out to the backyard. He cracked the bottle open and turned it up, swigging champagne as he walked over to the pool.

He felt like jumping in and sinking to the bottom. That would be useless, though, because he could swim like a fish. Besides, suicide wasn't his style. Mentally, he was stronger than that. He was hurting like hell, but not that bad.

He sank down on one of the lounge chairs and took another chug from the bottle. Perhaps he wasn't going to drown in the pool, but surely he could drown his sorrows in that bottle of Ace. He flopped back and looked upward. There he sat, watching the sun set over Los Angeles, alone and quiet.

It wasn't long before the bottle was empty. His emotions were still afloat, though, so he decided to start in on the Hennessy. He was going to need something a little stronger than champagne to numb this kind of pain. He went back inside the house, to the den area, where his bar was. Time to bring out the big guns, the dark liquor. He poured himself a shot of Henny, then another, and then a third. He slammed the glass down on the bar as the bittersweet taste of liquor numbed his senses.

He sat there silent, but being an intellectual, his mind was a blur, a hurricane of questions and emotions. He asked himself a thousand whys and whats. What could he have done differently? Why him? What did he do to deserve this? He'd just shared the news of their proposal with his father, right after he gave his father advice on how to maintain the relationship with his mother. Now it was Phil who needed someone to talk to, instead of folks always coming to him for a listening ear. He certainly couldn't call up his father. If he knew Phil's current situation, that he'd lost his fiancée before she even had a chance to become his wife, he'd probably start to question the advice he had gotten from Phil.

"Fuck!" Phil yelled. In his mind's eye, he looked over his and Denise's relationship. He had made her a priority, had introduced her to his family, and they'd all spent time together often. They took trips, and he did surprise her with really nice gifts sometimes. She was the only woman he had been with since they became exclusive. Even with all the temptation and the many opportunities, he had never dipped out on her. He literally had sex offered to him every day, and still he did what he was supposed to do, which was what all women only hoped and prayed their man would do: reject temptation. He saved all his lovin' for her.

The fact that Denise had left Phil a Dear John letter was chipping away at his ego. He truly thought he was doing everything to please this woman. He was attentive and made it a point to show his appreciation for the woman that she was. Hell, he was certain that he wasn't lacking in the bedroom. Their sex life was bananas. She always came a few times, outside of the lunch-time quickies. He knew that to be true, because every time she did, it had a sweet and distinct scent. On top of that, he had memorized the different ways she could cum, the way she dug her nails into his skin when she did, and the way she would tighten herself around him like a boa constrictor. Phil knew her body like Google Maps, plus, he was working with some nice-size equipment, so it couldn't have been a size thing either. Phil was blessed in that department and he knew it. He could barely hide the print of his endowment in his dress pants, so that damn sure wasn't it.

He thought about how he had challenged himself to be more creative and thoughtful in their relationship. He'd enrolled them in salsa classes once a week, and they were beginning to get good at it, too. Phil had taken classes and gotten his massage therapist license, complete with the big, professional table, because he wanted to be able to give Denise spa-quality treatment at home. He was a decent singer, too, so he had learned her favorite songs so he could sing them to her. All of this was to show her, through his actions, that she was important and a priority; that she was number one and there were no numbers two, three, or four.

The Henny had kicked in, and although he was still hurting, it didn't sting as much at the moment. In fact, the more he thought about her not appreciating his efforts and throwing it all away, the angrier it made him. He wasn't perfect, but he damn near had a cape on. Here he was, doing everything in his power to make her happy, and it still wasn't enough.

Phil got up from the bar to head to his backyard. Just in case the numbness wore off at some point, he poured one last glass for the road.

Back out in the yard, Phil looked around at his own private little island that was blocked on all sides by trees and fencing. This had come in handy on the nights that he and Denise had made love by the pool. The privacy came in handy again on this night, because without much thought, he took off all his clothes, grabbed his glass of Hen, and got in the hot tub. He turned it on high, set the timer for an hour, and lay back. As he watched the night sky, the stars and the moon were staring right back at him.

Phil thought about calling up his best friend and telling him what had happened. Being a therapist, Marc could give him not only some best-friend advice, but some professional advice as well. However, Phil was used to being the one who heard other people's issues and problems. He wasn't quite ready to have the tables turned on him right now, so he decided against placing the call. Besides, Marc's best-friend advice would probably be to tell him that the best way to stop the pain would be to find another woman to sleep with right away. That was the last thing Phil needed right now.

Phil soaked for a little while longer, and when he finally stood up, he felt the full effect of the alcohol he'd consumed. Standing there, naked in the night air, he looked like a statue, a drunk one. He hadn't had that much to drink in years, but it was okay. He was at home. It wasn't like he had to try to drive home in this condition. He was so buzzed that even walking might have been an issue.

Phil gathered his clothing and headed in the house. He piled the clothes on the counter next to the wine rack.

Glancing at the bottle of Apothic Red, he flashed back to the weekend he and Denise had driven to Napa Valley to do wine tasting. They'd stayed in an amazing resort, which was close to the best vineyards and restaurants. What made the trip even better was that there were barely any other guests there, so they pretty much had the full run of the place. They experienced the intimacy of couple's massages when they hit the spa. They went for incredible sunset walks. The romantic vibe led to some great times in the bedroom, too. They made love at least twice a day on that trip, and even made time for some downright fucking.

Phil thought back to how he'd caught Denise in the shower and snuck in behind her. He put his hands under the water before he touched her, so his hands wouldn't be cold, then he slid them down her body. She was sexy; she was sex.

He pressed his chest to her back, guided her legs open, and she snatched a breath as he eased himself inside her. She held the wall for stability as she took his strokes, each one deeper than the last.

Phil turned her toward him, wrapped her right thigh around him, and went back to work. Denise had been into fitness and yoga for years, so when Phil grabbed that same leg by the ankle and put it straight up in the air, she didn't flinch. She was in a standing split, and he tongue-kissed her feverishly as she came. Phil slowed the tempo a little, never stopping as he lowered her foot to his chest. He had never been one of those foot-fetish guys, but even he had to admit that Denise had some pretty-ass feet. Weekly pedicures were to be credited for such.

Phil pulled out for a moment but kept her where she was. He grabbed her Victoria's Secret Love Spell body wash and poured some on the foot he was holding. Gazing in her eyes as he washed her foot, he caught the look of pleasant surprise on her face. Neither one of them said anything as he rinsed the body wash off her foot. Phil slowly raised her foot to his mouth and kissed it. He could see this was turning her on. He had never done this to anyone, but why not her? He loved her, she was the best lover he'd ever had, and her foot was freshly washed.

Denise's eyes rolled back, and she leaned her head back against the wall as Phil began to gently suck her toes. Without missing a beat, he placed himself back inside her with a strong, slow stroke. It didn't take long before Denise had an orgasm that shook her body to the core. She gripped the wall like she was going to pull some of the tiles off of it. Phil had to put her foot down and catch her so she didn't fall. They sat down on the bench in the shower, laughing at themselves.

Phil didn't realize it, but the memory of that weekend actually had him smiling. He didn't want to be, but he was. *Those were some great times*, he thought. Some of the best days of his life.

He noticed that he was still naked and figured that he should probably do something about that. He went upstairs and showered. He was doing fine, until he noticed the body wash and the loofah in the shower. It was Love Spell, the same one they'd used on that Napa Valley trip. Against his better judgement, he opened it and smelled it.

It smelled like all the good things in life, and just like that, a rush of emotion came back to him: the sadness, the frustration, and the confusion. He wanted answers, more than some one- or two-paragraph letter could supply.

He hung his head, placed both hands on the shower wall, and let the water run down his face as he cried like he hadn't done since he was a child. He was hurt and angry and had to let it out. He felt he had done everything he could to make his relationship work, to no avail.

Phil stayed in the shower until he felt like he had gotten it all out of his system. Then he dried off, put on some comfortable boxer-briefs, and headed to sleep.

Phil didn't even make it all the way into the bed before Denise's smell on the pillows and sheets stopped him in his tracks. He pulled everything off the bed and put it in the hamper. He sprayed Febreze on the pillows and checked them, but they still smelled like her. Realizing that this wasn't going to be a quick thing, getting rid of the scent of the woman he loved, and that he was going to have to wash it all tomorrow, Phil put on some sweatpants and a wife-beater, grabbed a spare pillow and blanket, and headed downstairs to the couch. After he had used half a bottle of air freshener, the sofa no longer reminded him of her, so he lay down and tried to get some rest. Rest didn't come easy, let alone sleep, but somehow he made it through the night.

An idle mind is the devil's playground, and Phil was not going to let this situation overtake him. He'd seen this exact thing happen to many of his patients, which landed some of them in a deep depression that it took multiple sessions of counseling, and sometimes meds, to pull them out of. With that thought in mind, Phil spent the rest of the weekend cleaning, washing, and removing anything that smelled like or reminded him of Denise. This kept him quite busy, leaving very little downtime to replay their relationship and his loss over and over again in his mind.

He came across the credit card statement from the month before. That was when he'd purchased the engagement ring. He put both items in the cabinet. He'd have to return it soon, just not right now. It was safe to say that deep within, some hope still resided.

Monday morning came, and even though he didn't feel much like going to work, Phil knew it would help keep his mind off everything if he was busy, just as it had done over the weekend. He'd been so active, in fact, that there was nothing left to clean. It looked as though Rosa, his weekly cleaning lady, wouldn't need to come.

Even though Phil ultimately decided to go to work, he'd lain in bed for another fifteen minutes after his alarm went off. Within that fifteen minutes, he'd picked up his phone at least five times, preparing to call off work. Good thing he hadn't. As he finally arrived in his office an hour before his first appointment, Julie informed him that Marc was late for his 10:00 a.m. session.

"You think you can fill in for Marc and see Mr. Adams?" Julie asked Phil in a whisper. She eyeballed the gentleman sitting across the lobby, reading the newspaper.

Phil looked over his shoulder. He always arrived early so that he could take the time to go over some files and make notes prior to his own counseling sessions. Taking Marc's client would mean he wouldn't get a chance to do that. By the same token, things were already looking bad for Marc as far as the board was concerned. Phil couldn't leave his boy hanging out to dry like that. He turned back to face Julie then exhaled.

"Sure. Give me five and then send him in."

"I'll give you ten," Julie said as she whipped a folder from her desk and extended it to Phil. "It's his case file. I figured you might want to go over it, so I retrieved it from Marc's office." She'd never had any doubts that he would fill in for his best friend.

Phil nodded and then headed to his office, understanding now that his coming to work after all was a good thing. If he hadn't, Marc could have been out of a job.

While Phil got situated, Julie informed Mr. Adams that Marc's well-respected colleague would be seeing him today. Julie also gave him the option of rescheduling if he wasn't comfortable with that. Mr. Adams didn't seem to mind one way or the other as Julie led him into Phil's office.

"Phil, Mr. Adams to see you," Julie said as the patient walked through the open door to Phil's office.

Phil closed the case file he'd been glancing over and then stood to greet the older gentleman. Mr. Adams stood about six feet tall, had a bald head, grey beard, and the same dark brown complexion as Marc. The man could have easily passed for Marc's uncle.

"Good afternoon, Mr. Adams. Come in and have a seat," Phil said.

Mr. Adams sat down in the area right in front of Phil's desk with two comfortable leather chairs, a matching sofa, and an oak coffee table. On the table was a hand-carved marble chess set, complete with an antique board. Mr. Adams noticed it but fought to keep from appreciating it. He didn't want to be there, and it was written all over his face.

In going through Mr. Adams' file, Phil had noticed a few key things that may be helpful in his session, so he'd jotted them down. Mr. Adams was serving a court-ordered year of probation, which included one monthly, mandatory therapy session. It seemed Mr. Adams had some problems with road rage and anger management. According to Marc's half-ass notes, the patient had never revealed too much about himself in these forced sessions. Not one word. Technically, he didn't have to. Just as long as he showed up and stayed the entire hour, he got credit for the sessions—and, of course, Marc got paid for them.

Phil had read that he was a jazz musician. He played the saxophone, piano, and drums, but the horn was his baby. He had toured with some of the greats, and from his demeanor, Phil could tell that he felt belittled by having to come here. He resented it; hence, the silence.

Phil knew that a musician's mind was a different one. Their thinking process was heavy on the creative side, and they were definitely thinkers. Music was a language of its own. Most musicians liked to be challenged intellectually or they would get bored quick. Phil had seen the way Mr. Adams was looking everywhere in the room but at that chess board, a clear sign of what was really on his mind. He wasn't going to talk, but if properly persuaded, he just might indulge in a game. That would be Phil's way in.

Phil pressed play on a jazz playlist he had made a while back. He, too, was an intellectual and listened to everything from jazz to classical, from Tupac to Frank Sinatra.

Mr. Adams' ears perked up when he heard the first few bars of "Freddie Freeloader" by Miles Davis. He didn't know it, but he had already lost. He was dealing with a pro, and Phil was going to get Mr. Adams to interact with him.

Phil got up from his desk and came around to sit across from Mr. Adams. The only thing separating them was the table and the chess board. Knowing Marc, he had probably just sat at his desk, on Facebook, during his sessions with Mr. Adams.

Miles had Mr. Adams' nose open, and when Phil saw him sneak a peek at the craftsmanship of the marble chess pieces, he knew it was time to make a move.

"You play?" Phil asked.

Mr. Adams looked at Phil, at the board, then out the window.

"Mr. Adams, look, I know that you do not want to be here. I'm not going to try to force you or trick you into talking to me, but being that you have to be here and we just so happen to have a very nice board in front of us with even finer pieces, I think it would be a waste if we didn't at least have a game."

Mr. Adams looked Phil in the eye, then looked down to the game. He was considering the offer.

"I'll even let you pick which color you want."

He was motionless for a moment. Then, without saying a word, Mr. Adams reached out and turned the board so that he would be using the gray marble pieces and Phil would be black. In Phil's eyes, this was indeed progress.

"Bang Bang" by Dizzy Gillespie came on next. This song struck a chord with Mr. Adams, because he almost smiled, until he caught himself and put his poker face back on. Phil pretended not to see the moment, but he had. That's what made him good at what he did. It was always about the patient, what they did and didn't do, said and didn't say.

Mr. Adams moved his pawn two spaces forward, and the game was on. He didn't even realize that his uncomfortable scowl was gone, but once again, Phil had noticed. Back and forth they went. Phil could see that Mr. Adams knew his stuff. He thought that Mr. Adams was probably one of those older cats that played speed chess in the park while telling stories. He most likely had a board that he took with him on the road. Yeah, Phil could play chess online, but the real old-school dudes liked the feel of the pieces and the sounds they made when you moved them.

"So you're really going to just sit here and play, and not try to get me to talk?" Mr. Adams finally spoke.

"Yep. This board doesn't see a lot of action, and I figure if you want to talk to me about what happened, or about anything, you will."

"Maybe next session," he said as he took Phil's knight with his bishop.

Phil kindly took one of his pawns in return, just to let Mr. Adams know that he wasn't going to be an easy win, not was he going to just let him win. Mr. Adams was going to have to beat him, which was exactly the type of game he wanted.

At 11 a.m. on the dot, Julie chimed in on the intercom. "Dr. Gooden, your eleven o'clock appointment is here."

Phil looked at Mr. Adams. "I can put this up if you want to finish this game."

"Okay. I got you on the run. We can play it out next time."

"Sounds great. See you then."

Mr. Adams let himself out of the office as Phil put the chessboard on top of the bookshelf. He felt a sense of accomplishment for having made a breakthrough, even though it was a small one. Who knows? Maybe next time Mr. Adams would talk even more. Either way, Phil knew he was going to have to take over the Adams case. He was sure Marc wouldn't mind.

He looked at his appointment schedule to see who was next. Good old Mr. Egan. Phil grabbed his file out of the cabinet. It was always an adventure with this patient. Phil wondered what today held for him as he laughed a little.

Phil buzzed Julie on the intercom and said, "Please send in Mr. Egan."

He leaned back in his chair, thinking, *Here we go.* . . .

# Chapter 4

"Mr. Egan, good morning," Phil said as his next patient, and one of the more colorful ones, entered his office.

"Oh, no, my brother, it's been a great morning." The forty-year-old Charlie Sheen knock-off walked over to the couch as if he owned the place. He flopped down, stretched out his legs, crossing his ankles, and folded his hands across his stomach. Mr. Egan referred to it as "assuming the position."

Ever since his first session four months ago, he'd had the stereotypical visual in his mind that he was supposed to lay out on a couch and pour out his life story to the shrink while the shrink took notes. Even though ninety percent of Phil's patients never even sat on the couch, let alone lay on it, he never shared that fact with Mr. Egan. So what if he looked like a corpse lying there? If that's what it took to get the man to talk about his issues, then so be it.

Phil rested his forehead in his hand and then washed his hand down his face.

"You know me, Mr. Egan. I don't sugarcoat things. I won't be of any good to you if I do. I've been counseling you on the same problem for the last two years, and you cheat more now than you did when you came to see me. I am beginning to think that you don't want to change."

"But I do," he insisted.

Phil wanted to believe him, but didn't. Mr. Joseph Egan was the Bradley Cooper of corporate America: handsome, well dressed, six foot two, blond hair, blue eyes, and he couldn't keep his dick in his pants to save his life. He had boasted to Phil about living out every possible fantasy with two, three, and even four women at the same time, all this while being married. It was dangerous, selfish, and irresponsible, and Phil had told him so.

It wasn't that Phil was in any way jealous of him, nor did he want Mr. Egan's adventures. He genuinely wanted to help this man make his marriage work, but for whatever reason, Mr. Egan couldn't—or better yet, wouldn't—be faithful. He was only in counseling in the first place because his wife gave him an ultimatum: therapy or divorce.

So, there they were.

Mr. Egan sat there taking his scolding like a deserving child.

Phil exhaled, knowing that he truly had his work cut out for him. "Can I speak frankly for a moment, Mr. Egan?"

Mr. Egan nodded. "Sure."

"I'm going to invent the Fidelity Patch, a tamper-proof adhesive patch that your wife can stick on your ass every day, so you won't be able to get it up until she takes it off with a special remover."

Mr. Egan looked unsure of how to react to this idea.

"You tell me all the time that you have a great situation at home, but you're always in the streets looking for that rush you get when you sleep with a new woman. You said your wife will do anything physically to satisfy you, correct?"

"Correct."

"Then why do you feel the need to cheat?"

Mr. Egan thought for a moment and then shrugged. "I guess because I'm a 'lale,' if you will. A lesbian male. I just love women. All shapes, all sizes." He began using his hands to create figures and silhouettes. "Speaking of which, your office manager is pretty damn hot. Are you hittin' that?"

Phil stared at his patient for a moment, not even justifying his question with a response. In all of Mr. Egan's craziness, Phil could tell the man was dead serious. "Do you honestly want to stop cheating? All bullshit aside. We can't fix this if you aren't going to take it seriously. Do you love your wife, Mr. Egan, and just want to be with her and her alone?"

Mr. Egan could tell Phil wasn't playing around with him. "Well, yeah, yes." He turned his head away for a moment, seemingly in thought. He turned back to Phil and said, "I do, Doc."

"Okay then." Phil leaned back and exhaled. "We are going to start small. Do you think you can make it a week without cheating?"

Mr. Egan sighed. "Whew. A week? I don't know. That's a long time."

"Mr. Egan!" Phil said. "Just a week. Seven days. You mean to tell me you're that weak that you can't go seven days?"

Mr. Egan could hear the doubt and frustration in Phil's tone, but what he also heard, loud and clear, was Phil questioning whether he was weak. He was a man—a strong man. He was going to prove that he wasn't weak. "Okay, a week," he said with as much confidence as he could muster.

"Good. And that means no contact in any way, with any woman other than your wife, for the next seven days. You got that?" Phil spoke with authority.

"Okay," Mr. Egan said reluctantly, settling his body back against his chair. Then suddenly he perked up. "But what about guys?"

Phil's eyes nearly shot out of his head. This would call for a whole other type of session plan.

Mr. Egan burst out laughing. "I'm kidding, Doc. Calm down." When he realized Phil wasn't laughing with him, he stopped and got serious. "All right, you got it, Doc. A week."

Phil shook his head. Mr. Egan was too much. Not one to give up and quit on anything in life, however, Phil was bound and determined to help his client save his marriage.

Then it hit him: the same way he was willing to get through to Mr. Egan, perhaps he should use those same efforts to get through to Denise. It was possible that she was only experiencing cold feet. Maybe a talking to would cure her anxieties. Even though her letter said that she just wanted him to let her be, there was a chance that in all actuality, she wanted him to come after her. Women were funny like that sometimes. He'd learned that from some of his female patients, not to mention a couple of his exes with whom he'd experienced the whole on again/off again thing. Besides, hadn't he and his father just talked about fighting for what they wanted? Maybe it was time he put on his gloves and stepped into the ring.

Unfortunately, Phil felt doubt creeping in around the edges of his newfound resolve to win Denise back. He realized that he'd already been in the ring, and he had been knocked out. Before he let his mind wander too far into the depths of self-doubt, he forced himself to focus on Mr. Egan again. He'd be doing his patient a disservice otherwise, and if Phil was anything, he was a professional.

For the remainder of the session, Phil tried his best to stay focused on Mr. Egan's relationship and not his own. In all his years of practicing, Phil had never allowed issues in his personal life to intrude on his professional life. But then again, Phil's life hadn't really had too many issues to cause such distractions. He hadn't had the perfect life, but if he ever became famous and BET or TV One did one of those documentaries on him, he imagined it would be pretty boring. No stories about an absentee father, the death of a parent, drug use, or any of those other demons and dark clouds that coincidently seemed to lurk in the shadows of each celebrity biography. Just the opposite, Phil had lived a pretty damn good, drama-free life, up until Friday anyway. Actually, he thought, now he did have a dark cloud following him, one that could possibly keep him from ever wanting to love again.

"Well, Doctor, as always you've been a great help," Mr. Egan said as his session with Phil ended and he headed for the door.

"Have I really been a great help?" Was this doubt in his professional skills creeping into Phil's thoughts?

"Hell, yeah," Mr. Egan said emphatically. "I was supposed to swing by Rachel's after leaving here, but after talking to you, I think I'm going to stop by the flower shop, get my wife some flowers, and surprise her on the job."

"Rachel?" Phil questioned, then realized he didn't really want to hear about another one of Mr. Egan's side chicks. He waved his hand and said, "Never mind." Choosing to look at the glass as half full, Phil would stay focused on the good news that no matter who she was, Rachel would not be getting a piece of Mr. Egan today. Instead, he was going to do something nice for his wife. That was a good thing. Phil was finally starting to get through to this patient. It was indeed baby steps with this guy, but at least this was movement in the right direction. "I'm glad to hear of your revised plans, and I'm sure your wife will appreciate it."

"Yeah, I can't wait to see the look on her face. I think the last bouquet of flowers she held was at our wedding." He laughed. "I'd better get going. Can't keep Rachel waiting." He opened the office door.

"You mean your wife," Phil corrected him.

"Huh?" Mr. Egan said, his hand still on the knob as he looked back at Phil.

"You said you can't keep Rachel waiting. You meant you can't keep your wife waiting."

"Oh, no, I meant Rachel."

Phil looked perplexed. "You just said that instead of going to see Rachel you were going to take flowers to your wife's job." No way this dude had forgotten so quickly.

"I am going to take my wife flowers first," Mr. Egan clarified. "Then I'm going to see Rachel." He winked and then trotted out the door as Phil's countenance fell into a frown—until Mr. Egan threw over his shoulder, "Just kidding, Doctor Gooden. Just kidding." He began laughing. "I'll see you next week, Doc."

Phil let out a gust of wind. Mr. Egan had him going there for a minute. He had jokes for days. Phil wrote down a few things in his case file then stood up and placed it in the file cabinet behind his desk.

Julie peeked her head into Phil's office. "Hey, Batman, thought you might like to know that Robin finally showed up."

"Huh? What?" Phil asked, closing the drawer then turning to face Julie.

"Dr. Collins is here," Julie explained. Noticing that something seemed off about Phil, she asked, "You okay? Your mind seemed to be off somewhere else. That's not like you."

It didn't surprise Phil that Julie could notice just the slightest difference in his usual demeanor. She was perceptive like that. Heck, she might have made a good therapist if she went back to school and got her degree. That still didn't mean he wanted to open up to her about Denise leaving. It might have been nice to talk to someone about his feelings, but he knew all about that whole "letting your guard down" thing and where that kind of vulnerability might lead him and Julie. He wasn't going to take that chance with Julie right now, because as far as he was concerned, it was not definitely over with Denise yet.

He cleared his throat and feigned a chuckle. "Yeah, I'm good. You know how it is with that Mr. Egan."

Julie rolled her eyes up in her head. "Do I ever. I don't know who's worse when it comes to flirting, him or Dr. Collins."

"Speaking of Dr. Collins . . ." Phil was glad his efforts to change the subject had worked. "I better go talk to him real quick. Let me know when my next client arrives." He hurried past Julie, not wanting her to be able to read into his actions any more than she already had.

Julie stepped to the side to let him by. "And you might want to take him an iron. Boy looks like he slept in his clothes."

Phil threw his hand up as he walked toward Marc's office, signaling to Julie that he would handle it. *Same shit, different day*, he thought.

# Chapter 5

"So I see you finally decided to show up," Phil said as he walked into Marc's office.

"Oh, yeah, my bad, man," Marc said as he fiddled around with a file on his desk, avoiding eye contact with Phil. "Julie told me you saw Mr. Adams for me. 'Preciate it."

"Well, I'd appreciate you showing up to work on time." Phil's voice went from calm to bitter as he closed Marc's office door behind him. "Did our talk on Friday go in one ear and out the other or what?" Phil snapped. "This is bullshit. I'm starting to think you're taking my friendship for granted and that you don't give a fuck about me or this company." Phil was spitting fire.

Marc was definitely taken aback. This just wasn't the way Phil ordinarily communicated . . . with anybody. "I said my bad, man." Marc raised his hands in defense.

"My bad! This ain't no 'my bad' type situation." Phil continued on his rant. "Your livelihood is at stake. Do you not enjoy the ability to pay your bills and put food on the table? And even if you don't, what about me?" Phil poked at his own chest. "I have a lot at stake. I love you like a brother. I will have your back no matter what, but not at the expense of my career and my license. If you know what's good for you, you will get your shit together, buy an alarm clock and an iron, and have your ass at work doing what you're supposed to do when you're supposed to do it."

When he recovered from his shock, Marc tried to lighten the mood by saying, "You done?" He let out a chuckle.

"Damn, Marc, can you be serious for just five seconds of your life?" Phil slammed his fist down on the file Marc had been reviewing. That wiped the grin right off of Marc's face. If he hadn't taken his best friend seriously a moment ago, he sure as hell knew that he meant business now.

"I'm sorry, man. Seriously." Marc's sincere tone matched his claim. He rose from his seat. "I messed up."

Phil shot him a glare, not ready to accept his apology that quickly.

Marc spoke up to fill the angry silence between them. "Okay, I've been messing up," he admitted. "I've never been one to take life so seriously like you have. It's a hard habit to break. But you're my dude. You go to bat for me, and I understand you have a lot at stake. I owe you better."

"Then do better," Phil said in a less than sympathetic tone. This was the first time Marc actually did sound convincing, but Phil was done playing games. Maybe the rest of the world liked playing games and taking his kindness for granted, but that wasn't the type of person he was—and he was starting to have less and less respect for people who did.

"I will, man. That's a promise. Not only do I not want to lose this job, but I don't want to lose our friendship either. Cool?" Marc extended his hand to Phil, who ignored the gesture of a peace offering. "We cool?" Marc asked again, stretching his hand even more.

After a couple of seconds, Phil relented and shook it. "We're cool."

Marc exhaled, relieved, then went and sat back down at his desk. He looked slightly broken, like a kid who had disappointed his dad. Unlike Phil, Marc actually did lack a father figure in his life, so over the years, not only had Phil played the role of best friend and big brother in Marc's life, but on occasion he'd had to play Dad and lay down the law with tough love, like he'd just done.

Phil had to admit to himself that in their entire friendship, he'd never come at Marc as sideways as he had just now. Unfortunately for Marc, he had to bear the brunt of all the emotions Phil was suppressing.

"Look, I'm sorry I was talking to you like that, cussing and carrying on," Phil said. "You know that's not how I do things." As a trained therapist, Phil knew that yelling and cussing at a person will only cause that person to shut down.

"It's okay."

"It's not, because if you ever talk to me like that, we gon' rumble," Phil warned in a joking manner.

"I hear you." Marc nodded.

"But I really do need this to be the last time I speak with you about work," Phil reiterated. "You have to do better, because I know you are better. I would have never put my neck on the line for you if I didn't believe in you."

"I know, man, and it's not the first time you've put yourself out there on the line for me either. I appreciate it."

"Well, I'm glad you recognize it."

"I do," Marc said, "and I also recognize that me being late is not the real reason why you came at me like that. What's really going on?"

Upon first instinct, Phil thought to play Marc the same way he'd played Julie when she inquired about his behavior. But wasn't he the one who claimed he didn't play games? It was time to be real, and if he couldn't be real with his best friend, then who could he be real with? His best friend of twenty years could see right through him, and Phil knew it.

Phil exhaled deeply and then grabbed the chair across from Marc. He came right out and announced, "Denise is gone."

Marc stared at him, speechless, for a moment. "I didn't know she'd been here." He looked at his watch. "Is it lunchtime already?" Marc was aware that Denise would come to the office a couple times a week to have lunch with Phil.

"No, man, she wasn't here. I mean, she was here, but— Man, she left me. We're not together anymore. She's gone as in gone out of my life."

Once again, Marc stared at his friend. He was waiting for the punchline. This had to be a joke. Just last month Phil had told him he was going to buy the woman in his life an engagement ring, and he'd actually gone out and done it. "For real?" Marc had to be sure before he spoke any more words.

"For real," Phil assured him.

"Damn, I'm sorry, bro," Marc said sincerely.

Phil appreciated his friend's empathy.

"What happened? What the hell did you do to mess things up with her?" Marc asked.

Phil shot him a look. "What did I do? Nothing . . . except give her everything but the moon."

Marc shook his head. "Then maybe you should have given her the moon. A bad-ass broad like that deserves the moon."

Phil shot darts at Marc with his eyes.

"What?" Marc shrugged his shoulders. "I'm just saying. If you've already given someone everything, why stop when you get to the moon?"

"Look, I did everything in my power to make her a priority, not only with words, but I backed it up with action: flowers, trips, time, affection, love, friendship, communication, massages, multiple orgasms. You name it, I did it!" Phil looked away and blew out an angry breath. "Anyway, I don't want to go into it right now. Not here at work."

"Okay, cool." Marc knew not to push the issue and pry further. "Well, on another note, when are you gonna teach me how to do that hypnotizing thing?"

"I'm not," Phil said.

"Why?"

"'Cause knowing you, you'll be around here trying to hypnotize your female patients to sleep with them."

Marc held a serious look on his face. "And . . .?"

Phil laughed. "My point exactly." He continued, taking their conversation back to the place where it had started. "Don't take this the wrong way, but you don't take this job as seriously as you should."

"I'm just being me, man. I'm not going to change who I am because I am a doctor now."

"And I'm not saying you should. I'm saying you have to separate the two. You are a doctor from nine to five. After five, be as wild as you want to be. Just don't let it affect your work. And stop banging your patients."

"I only slept with one of my patients," Marc said. "This week."

"See what I'm talking about?"

"Point taken. Point taken," Marc said.

"All right then. I'll holler at you later."

"We watching the game at Kareem's house tonight. You wanna roll?"

Phil though for a moment. Even though hanging with the fellas might have taken his mind off of Denise, even if just for a couple of hours, he simply wasn't up to it. "Nah, another time. I have some work to do." Phil turned to leave.

"All right, but if you change your mind, hit me."

"I will," Phil assured him. He went to exit Marc's office.

Julie happened to be standing right outside of it with her hand raised to knock. "Oh, hey, I was just coming to get you," Julie said to Phil. "Your next appointment just called and said he wouldn't be able to make it today. I left the message on your desk."

"Thanks, Julie," Phil said.

"No problem," she said, giving Phil a comforting smile then walking away.

"Mmmm, mmm, mmm," Marc said as he watched Julie walk away. "If only I could get her to look at me that way."

"What way?" Phil asked, feigning stupid. Of course he noticed how Julie looked at him.

"The way she looks whenever she's talking to you," Marc answered. "You know, with all that seduction and mystery behind her eyes." Marc started making googly eyes.

"Marc . . ." He paused. "You stupid," Phil said before turning to leave.

"No, you stupid if you can't see it for yourself," Marc said. "You know, there's that saying about God closing one door."

Phil looked to Marc to finish his thought.

"He closes one door and opens another, and if I'm not mistaken, didn't you just open the door?"

Phil thought for a second and then answered. "As a matter of fact I did, and now I'm closing it." Phil closed the door in Marc's face and then headed to his office, all the while wondering if his best friend, for the first time in his life, had spoken words that might have actually made sense.

Realizing that with the cancellation, his next patient wouldn't be coming for a while, Phil decided to walk to the sushi spot not far from the office. He stopped by

Julie's desk on his way out to see if she wanted anything, but she wasn't there, so he headed out.

Phil made it back to his office with plenty of time to eat his lunch and catch up on some paperwork. He had grabbed a spicy tuna roll and a California roll for Julie, just in case she hadn't eaten. She was on a call when he walked up to her desk, and he could tell by the salty expression on her face when she looked at his carry-out bag that she had yet to eat. Her look of surprise when he pulled out the items he had gotten for her and set them in front of her, was even more priceless.

Phil didn't say a word. He just smiled, nodded as if to say "you're welcome," and went in to his office. He could feel her watching him as he walked away, so he looked back, just so she would know that he was aware of what she was doing.

*And she had better be careful*, he thought. He was single now, and she was far too fine to be flirting with him.

Phil finished his lunch and his paperwork right on time. He figured that any second now, Julie would buzz him and let him know that his patient was there. Phil straightened up his desk then looked around his office to make sure that everything was in place.

Right on cue, the intercom buzzed. It was Julie as expected, letting him know that his next patient had arrived.

"Send him in," Phil told her.

In walked William Reedy, a fifteen-year-old high-school student with some self-esteem and anger management issues. William was five foot four, 130 pounds. He dressed conservatively, as if he didn't want to stand out, always in browns, grays, or blacks. He rarely made eye contact, and he spoke in a loud whisper, like he was afraid of his own voice.

It had been well documented that William didn't think too highly of himself, but lately, it had gotten to a point of concern. He was being bullied at school, because he was quiet and kept to himself. According to his file, this had been going on for a while. His parents recently thought that it would be a good idea for him to see someone about the things that were going on, because he had brought a knife to school to protect himself from a boy who was harassing him every day. This was his third session.

William walked in and sat down in the same chair, with the same body language he usually projected: shoulders slumped, head down, hands clenched, and eyes glued to the floor. When he did occasionally bring his head up to look around and analyze the room and Phil, he would glance for a second then immediately look out the window.

Phil got up from his chair and went to sit closer to William. He didn't want to sit too close, so he sat right across from him, on the other side of the coffee table. This was intentional. Phil knew that this would make it very difficult to keep disconnecting from the conversation, like he usually did.

"How are you doing today, William?"

"Good."

William's answers were always short and uninformative, unless Phil got creative with the questions and made sure that they were open-ended and required more than one or two words to answer.

"Anything special, good or bad, happen in school today?"

"Well, I didn't get bothered by anybody, if that's what you're asking."

"Why do you think that is?"

"Probably because I brought a knife to school. Now everyone thinks that I'm crazy."

"Is that what you wanted, to be left alone?"

"Yes, but I didn't want to be ostracized. Now no one will talk to me, except for a couple other kids that Michael was bullying. I'm like a hero to them, for standing up to him."

Phil could tell that this young man was very smart, probably the type that got bored in class if the material wasn't challenging him. William's demeanor had shifted a little.

"So where do we go from here?" Phil asked. "How do we keep something like the knife incident from happening again?"

"That's what I was going to ask you. Aren't you supposed to have all the answers?"

"Actually, no. I'm not. I'm supposed to ask the right questions, to help us both figure out the answers."

Phil noticed a look of intrigue on William's face. He was being challenged, and something about it appealed to him.

"Were you actually going to use the knife on this Michael kid?"

"No. I just wanted him to stop bothering me. Every single day, he's on my back for no reason. He bumps me in the hallway, knocks my books out of my hand, messes with my food at lunch in the cafeteria, or talks about my clothes in front of the whole class. He even smacked my glasses off my face one day. I figured enough was enough."

"Was there any other way you could have resolved this, other than bringing a weapon to school?"

"I had been telling the teachers, the principal, and my counselor, but all they did was talk to the boy, and he got even worse after that. Plus, he's a star athlete, so he gets away with murder at school," William complained.

"Well, the good news is that people are actually leaving you alone now, right?"

"Yes, but the bad news is that Michael's running around the school now, telling everyone that I'm psycho. Can't win for losing." William's body language shifted again, he felt defeated and it showed.

As gently as he could, Phil pointed out, "You also know that they could have sent you to juvenile detention for what you did, right?"

"Yes. Apparently, if this doesn't go well, they still can."

"I wouldn't worry about that if I were you," Phil said with a smile. "I want to extend an invitation to you. First of all, before you leave, I'm going to give you my cell number. That way, if you are being bothered again, you can call me and I can come talk to the principal myself. Okay?"

"Yeah, but you and I both know that you can't fight all my battles for me."

"You are absolutely right, but I can show you how to fight your own. That way if he pushes you or hits you again, you can defend yourself. You won't need to bring anything. You will have your hands, and that's all you will need. Does that sound like something you want to do?"

"Yes. I'm tired of this whole thing, and if whatever you're going to show me can help, then I'm in." The tension in William's face had noticeably diminished.

"Okay, good. But what I show you is *only* for defending yourself. You have to promise me that you won't ever start a fight with it, just end one."

"I can handle that," William agreed.

Phil had boxed for a couple years when he was younger. He had also studied Krav Maga, so he was proficient in the art of self-defense and close quarter combat. He spent the rest of the session showing William some basic self-defense techniques. He also gave William's parents the number to the man who taught him martial arts, so they could enroll him in classes. Phil knew that a certain kind of peace of mind came with the ability to handle one's self.

Phil also knew that kids like William were usually the ones who were bullied to the point that they thought suicide or shooting up the school was the only option they had, and he would be damned if this young man was going to be another statistic.

# Chapter 6

A sullen and distraught-looking Latin woman burst out of Marc's office in tears. She stormed across the lobby, mumbling something in Spanish. Whatever she was saying clearly reflected her anger and hurt. Julie hurriedly looked down at the appointment book in search of the woman's name.

"Miss Quinton, wait," Julie said. She stepped around her desk but stopped on the side of it. She didn't get too close to the woman.

"What's going on out here?" Phil stepped out of his office, closing the door behind him. He made note of the sobbing woman standing in front of Julie's desk.

Placing his hand on Julie's shoulder, he asked, "Are you all right?"

Julie swallowed hard and nodded. "Yes, I'm good, but clearly Marc's patient, Miss Mariah Quinton, isn't."

"I'm so sorry for whatever happened, and I'm going to take care of whatever it is," Phil apologized in a whisper. He was hoping that if he spoke in a lowered tone then Miss Quinton would follow suit. Phil had a patient in his office that he didn't want walking out on him due to the unprofessional scene going on in the lobby. He was already embarrassed that he'd had to excuse himself.

Phil's patient was just getting to the meat of her issues, but all the yelling and door slamming had interrupted the session. Phil had to come out to not only see what was going on, but to make sure that Julie was safe as well.

"Just calm down, Mariah." It was company policy to call patients by their last names, but Phil made the call that in this case, he needed to make things personal. "I'm sure that you have a good reason to be as upset as you are." Phil waited until she made eye contact with him before continuing. "You don't look like the type of woman who would just fly off the handle for no reason."

Miss Quinton relaxed her shoulders and her mouth. She was starting to loosen up.

Phil shot Julie a quick glance. Julie twisted her lips, gave Phil a "don't look at me; you got this," look, and then swiveled her body right back down into her seat.

Julie just sat there, the corners of her mouth twisting up into a grin, watching the master at work. She felt secure that if anybody could diffuse this situation, Dr. Gooden could.

Phil turned his attention back to Miss Quinton. "Look, Mariah, I'm with a client right now, but once I finish up, if you'd like to talk—"

"Can't," she said, disappointed as she gazed starry-eyed at Phil. "I was here for my session with Dr. Collins on my lunch break. I don't have a full hour to spare."

"I hate to see a dissatisfied patient," Phil told her. "If you'd like, I can look into taking over your future sessions. Would you like that?" Phil didn't mean to come across as sensual as he had, but he couldn't help it.

Miss Quinton, speechless, couldn't do anything but nod.

"Good. Just go home, or go back to work rather. Get yourself together, then call Julie here to get you penned in on my calendar. But for now, I really need to get back to my patient. We can't have two patients in one day not pleased, now, can we?"

Through gloss-covered lips, Miss Quinton whispered, "No."

Phil smiled at the woman then looked to Julie. "Julie, let my next appointment know I'm running just a tad behind, will you?"

"Why certainly, Dr. Gooden," Julie said.

"And don't forget to put Miss Quinton's remaining sessions on my calendar." He looked up at Miss Quinton and winked. "Right, Mariah?"

Again, there was no response, just a nod as Phil headed back to his office.

Before closing the door behind him, he heard Julie say, "Well, Miss Quinton, looks like today was your last court-ordered session anyway."

Phil exhaled loudly as he closed the door behind him. He was relieved that he wouldn't have to do a one-on-one session with Miss Quinton after all. But on second thought, it concerned him. From what he had just witnessed, it looked like Marc hadn't made any headway with that woman. What really worried Phil was that underneath all that anger Mariah was displaying had to be some hurt and pain. Anger was just the mechanism she was using to cover it all up. Not only could Mariah end up being a danger to the rest of the world, but also a danger to herself.

"Everything okay out there, Dr. Gooden?" Phil's patient asked after he returned to the office.

"It is for now," Phil said as he walked back over to his desk. He sat down and returned his attention to his case-file. He stared at it for a moment, his mind wandering off. He hated that he'd already walked out on his patient once, but Miss Quinton's actions were bothering him. He couldn't imagine for the life of him what had ticked her off so much.

He looked up at his patient. "I really hate to do this, but can we reschedule today's session? There is a situation that I really need to get to the bottom of, and I don't want it to take away from your session. And since you are a private pay client, I'll waive the fee for your next session."

Although ninety percent of Phil's patients had insurance or their sessions were covered by the state, he had a couple who didn't fall under either of those categories but still needed help. Phil either undercharged them tremendously for his sessions, or did them pro bono. Yes, his profession paid well, but it wasn't all about the money. He truly did like helping people.

Once Phil's patient agreed to reschedule, he escorted her out of the office, stopped her at Julie's desk to make her next appointment, and then headed straight to Marc's office. It seemed like in the last week, Marc had been taking up a great deal of his time, and Phil was sick and tired of it. The board had scheduled a meeting with Phil for later in the month, and something told him the subject of Marc would be on the agenda.

The closer Phil got to Marc's office, the more enraged he became. He opened the closed office door without knocking, and was appalled at the sight before him. Gritting his teeth so tight that his jaw bones began to stiffen. He looked around for a moment, his eyes catching the mini refrigerator in Marc's office. Walking over to it, he opened it up and grabbed a bottle of water, twisted the cap off, and took a swig as he marched over to Marc's desk, where he turned the bottle upside down and poured the water out . . . on Marc.

"Oh, shit!" Marc jerked out of his slumber as the water hit his head. He extended his arms, trying to block the water, looked down at his wet shirt, then looked up at Phil, who was sipping the last bit of water from the bottle. "What the hell did you do that for?"

"Ahh," Phil said, drinking the rest of the water in the bottle and then setting it down on Marc's desk.

"What are you, crazy?" Marc stood up, brushing his hands down his shirt as if that would somehow magically dry it off.

"Actually, I must be crazy to keep giving you chances," Phil said. "So why don't you just go home?"

"I guess I'm going to have to," Marc said. "I can't see the rest of my clients looking like this." That's when something dawned on Marc. "My clients." He looked around the room. "Where is Miss Qu—"

"Mariah? She's gone!" Phil said. "But I guess if you fall asleep while a patient is pouring their heart out then you won't know that they've left your office." The more words Phil spoke, the louder his voice rose.

Marc looked down at himself once again. "I look a mess."

"Well, it would be a step up from what you usually look like."

"Look, I'm—"

"Sorry." Phil finished his best friend's sentence.

Marc looked up at the seriousness in his friend's expression. The usual disappointment wasn't present in Phil's eyes. This time Phil was flat out pissed.

"I'm going to go home and change," Marc said. "I'll be back."

"Don't bother," Phil said.

"What do you mean, don't bother? I can't stay here and—"

"Don't bother coming back," Phil clarified.

Marc stood there with his arms wide open, along with his mouth. He was in disbelief. Yeah, he knew he'd been messing up in these last couple of months, but he had his reasons, which he'd kept to himself. He tried to explain, "I'm going through some things just like you are. You should be able to understand."

"Yes, I'm going through some things," Phil admitted. "My girl left me, my parents are having problems, my best friend doesn't give a shit about himself or how he makes me look at work. So, hell yeah, I'm going through some things, but I still carry my ass in here every day—on time—and give these people the professional service they are entitled to." Phil was livid, and the veins in his forehead began to pop. "Except for today. I had to reschedule a client so I could handle whatever it is you have going on with Miss Quinton," Phil said, finally having to take a breather. He stood there with his chest going up and down because he was breathing so hard.

Marc extended his hand to reach out to his best friend, but then thought better of it. He'd screwed up one time too many. He couldn't expect his best friend to keep bailing him out. If Phil did decide to fire him, he deserved it, although he hoped things wouldn't come to that. Perhaps a couple days off was just what he needed to try to get his life in order. Without saying another word, Marc gathered his belongings and exited the office, leaving Phil standing there alone.

Suddenly standing there alone with his thoughts was tough for Phil. Since Denise had left him, he'd done everything imaginable to keep himself busy, wearing himself out so that by the time his head hit the pillow he'd be out like a light. Even his anger at Marc had been a welcome distraction from his more painful feelings of rejection and abandonment.

It had been almost two weeks since Denise had left him, and he was starting to come to terms with the fact that it might really be over. He knew women well enough to know that when they'd made up their mind, their mind was made up. He was starting to think that it would be better to accept that it was over and not to let the situation continue to occupy his mind.

"I saw Marc leaving."

Phil heard Julie's voice coming from the doorway.

"I was on a call so I couldn't talk to him," Julie continued. "Should I cancel his appointments for the day?"

Phil turned to Julie. "No, cancel them for the rest of the week," Phil said as he stared out the window.

"Well, if you need anything, you know I'm here," Julie said.

Phil looked at her. He nodded as he said, "Yeah, I know."

Julie smiled and then left Phil alone with his thoughts again.

"I know," he repeated to Julie, even though she was long gone. "You've always been here, Julie." And maybe, just maybe, it was time Phil appreciated that.

# Chapter 7

When the door opened, Phil didn't bother to invite himself in. He didn't know whether he'd be welcome, so he stood out on the porch in his gym shorts and a wife beater, and waited for Marc to set the tone. After a few seconds of pure silence, it felt too much like some urban, modern day standoff. Who was going to make the first move?

Realizing there would never be closure to the matter if both parties just stood there looking stupid, Phil looked down at the basketball that was cupped under his arm and then passed it to Marc.

Marc caught it and stood in the doorway kind of rolling it on his palm. The moment was awkward to say the least.

"Best three out of five," Phil said, looking at Marc, who was still in the boxers he'd slept in and a T-shirt that looked as though some of Marc's breakfast—or, knowing Marc, last night's dinner—might have taken residence there. "Go get some balling gear on. I'll meet you over at the court."

Marc stared down at the ball for a moment and then looked to his best friend, or perhaps his ex-best friend. The verdict was still out on that. He threw the ball back to him.

Phil couldn't tell from his body language alone whether Marc was game, so he took it upon himself to call the shots.

"Get your game clothes on," Phil repeated. "I'll meet you over at the park in ten minutes." Phil didn't wait on a response, because he knew he probably wouldn't get one this time either. He simply walked off the porch and headed down the walkway. On the sidewalk, he began dribbling the ball toward the park where he and Marc played on some Saturdays along with a few other of their mutual friends.

He didn't even have to look over his shoulder. He could feel Marc's eyes burning a hole through him. Eventually, he heard the door slam.

Marc was shutting him out, literally, but that didn't make Phil turn around, hop back in his car, and leave. With very little faith, he went to the court anyway and began taking shots. After fifteen minutes, when he'd worked up a sweat warming up and there was still no sign of Marc, he decided his efforts had been in vain. He took one last shot, half court, before deciding to return to his car.

"Show off," Phil heard someone call out as the half-court shot cleared the net.

He turned to look behind him and saw Marc standing there. He was geared up in his basketball fits, sweat bands and all, ready to go.

"You come to play or heckle?" Phil asked, relieved that Marc had actually shown up. There was hope after all. Way back in the corner of his mind, a part of him wondered if there was still the same hope for him and Denise. With her knowing that on Saturday mornings the court was Phil's stomping ground, was there a chance she might show up too?

"Actually, I came to whoop yo' ass," Marc said. He started walking toward Phil.

"Check," Phil said, bouncing the ball to Marc.

"Check." Marc nodded and then bounced it back. After that, it was on.

The two friends went at it on the court. It definitely wasn't a PG-13 game either, with pushing, fouls, hacking, trash talking, and more. This was a therapy session for both of them. They needed it. Phil knew that he did.

"Best two out of three," Phil said, breathing heavily after making the shot that won him one game of the two the men had already played. He hunched over with his hands on his knees, sweat pouring off his brow.

"Oh, no." Marc vigorously shook his head. "You came to my door, waking me up early in the morning, talking 'bout best three out of five like you Jordan or something. Naw, we're gonna go all five."

Phil looked up at Marc. "What you talking about early in the morning? It's noon." Early in the morning was when they would usually shoot hoops with the other guys. That was the best time to play ball, before the sun was really out for blood. It was late compared to their usual time, and Phil had no help on the court today. That was something he wished he'd thought about before.

They fought through the next two games, until it was tied at two apiece. Both men were exhausted. They had each finished their bottles of Gatorade a game ago, and neither of them was sure if they had one more game in them. Phil hadn't been sleeping well since the breakup with Denise, and Marc was hungover as usual, yet neither of them wanted to be the first to forfeit the fifth game.

Out of nowhere, Marc started laughing.

"What?" Phil looked around to see if he'd missed something. He couldn't figure out for the life of him just what was so funny.

Marc's laughter got louder, until it turned into a roar. Finally it became so contagious that Phil started laughing. Before either knew it, they were both sharing a hearty laugh, almost to the point of tears.

Phil looked over his shoulders. "Clearly, neither of us wants to say it, so I will. To hell with this last game. It's ninety degrees. I'm hot and tired." Phil sat down in protest. Marc was still laughing as he joined him.

Phil couldn't remember the last time he had laughed like that, and he realized now how much he had missed it. Lately, he had been feeling like he wasn't living a charmed life anymore, with Denise gone and his friendship with Marc under some serious strain. Sure women come and go, and so do friends, but both Denise and Marc were important factors in his life. Each were his best friend in different ways. They were the only two people, besides his parents, who he'd allowed to play such a big part of his life. As a matter of fact, he could share things with Denise and Marc that he wouldn't dare even share with his parents.

Since it was starting to look like he'd lost Denise for good, it probably made good sense for him to open up to the one best friend he had left, before he lost him too.

"I'm sorry, man," Phil said, his laughter dying down.

Marc cleared his throat, forcing his own laughter to a halt.

"I shouldn't have come at you the way I did in the office the other day," Phil said, though he was quick to add a disclaimer. "I'm not sorry for sending your ass home, though. It was long overdue and you know it."

"Apology accepted," Marc said, conspicuously leaving out any apology of his own for slacking off at work.

Phil chose to ignore that, and began to explain his own reasons for overreacting. "With the whole Denise situation going on and all, I think I probably took everything I was feeling out on you."

"Oh, yeah. You never did give me all the details about y'all's split," Marc said curiously.

"Yeah, that's another reason I came to see you this morning."

"Oh, you mean it wasn't just to get your ass beat in a game of B-ball?"

"You ain't beat nobody's ass. It's two games to two."

"That's because I felt sorry for you. I didn't want to take advantage of a man with a broken heart." Marc laughed while starting to dribble the ball. "But seriously, why don't you tell me what's up—but back at the house. This sun is cooking me."

Phil nodded in agreement, and they both got up, continuing their discussion as they walked toward Marc's house.

"Now that you're done with Denise, what's up with Julie?" Marc asked when they were back inside his home. "You know she has the hots for you."

"See, that's why I didn't call you when it first went down," Phil said, flopping down on the couch. "I knew the only advice you'd have for me was to find a replacement." Easier said than done, as Denise was irreplaceable in Phil's eyes.

Marc rolled his eyes but dropped the subject of Julie. "So tell me what happened with Denise."

Phil shook his head. "I don't know, man. One minute I was proposing to her at my office. She was saying 'I do.' I get home from work that very same day, and her and all of her stuff is gone. She left me a note."

"What'd it say?"

"Something about marriage scaring her, and she wasn't ready, and some other stuff."

"So why didn't she just tell you she wasn't ready? Let me guess: her ass wanted that ring. 'Cause y'all could have even just postponed the engagement and y'all would still be a couple. Why did she choose to leave though?"

"I don't know, man. Might have been something else other than that." For the first time since Denise had left Phil, another possible reason for her actions entered his mind. "Or somebody else." The thought of Denise being with another man made Phil cringe inside. It would hurt much more if that was the real reason she left.

"Then if that's the case, get you somebody else. Denise isn't the only woman out there." Marc was ready to get back to a discussion of Julie.

Obviously, Phil was not interested in taking the conversation in that direction. "Denise was different. She can't be easily replaced. You know that," he said.

"I know, I know," Marc said, relenting. "I just figured it's better to try to get you to laugh about it than having you sitting over there looking like you just lost your best friend." He frowned and pointed at him. "Kind of like you do now."

"She was my best friend. Other than your goofy ass. I would have done anything for that girl. Then she just ups and leaves. Doesn't even say good-bye. Not to my face anyway. Left me a damn Dear John letter." Phil took a swallow of his drink while Marc nearly choked on his.

"I'm sorry, bro, but a Dear John letter?" Marc said, steadily pouring salt into the wound. "I just can't get over that."

"*You* can't get over it. How do you think I feel?"

"She played you like that. No wonder you look like you were 'bout ready to cut your wrists. I would've done been did that if I were you. What a blow to an ego. Not only does your chick leave you, but she don't even give you any notice. She *Dear John*ed you like you ain't mean nothing. I'm talking—"

"All right, all right," Phil said, cutting off Marc's recap of his current situation.

Marc looked at his pitiful friend. "Well, did she at least give the ring back?"

"Yes, she did, but it's not about the ring."

"The hell it ain't," Marc snapped, standing up. "You know how much Mello down at the pawnshop would give for a diamond engagement ring?"

Phil sucked his teeth. "No, but I'm sure you would know. Besides, I still have time to take it back to the store." Phil shook his head. "I just don't know."

"What's not to know? Take it back and move on. It is what it is."

Phil stood. "You know what? Talking to you wasn't a good idea." Phil had told himself that with time, he would get through this, but hell, after talking to Marc, he sure didn't feel any better.

"No, no, I'm sorry." Marc waved him to sit back down. "My bad. Chill. Have a seat."

"Why? So I can wait here while you go get me the razor to cut my wrist?" Phil said sarcastically, though he reluctantly sat back down.

"No," Marc assured him, then jokingly added, "Unless I'm a beneficiary on your life insurance policy."

"You know what? You're an idiot. I'm gone." This time Phil stood to leave and made it to the door.

"No, hold up, for real. Because I'm just saying . . ." Marc chased after him. "You know there's a clause in them life insurance policies. They will payout for a suicide as long as the policy has been active for over two years."

Phil raised his hand to signal for Marc to shut up as he opened the front door. "Stop talking, Marc. I don't want to hear from you until Monday at work."

Phil's words took Marc into serious mode. "Wait. Did you say Monday at work? Because I thought I was—"

"You were warned," Phil said, standing on the porch. He stopped on the first step and turned to Marc. "I didn't turn in anything official. The board doesn't know about your little incident last week."

Marc took in Phil's words and was overwhelmed with gratitude. "Thanks, bro." He stepped outside and shook Phil's hand. "Good looking out."

"You know I got your back," Phil said. "But I'ma need you to have mine. Shape up or—" Although Phil couldn't fix his lips at the moment to say that he would fire Marc, he'd do it in a heartbeat if it came down to him or Marc. He'd worked too hard to get where he was.

"You don't even have to say it," Marc said.

"Good, then don't make me. I'm out."

"Take it easy," Marc said as Phil headed back to his car.

Phil got inside his car, turning on the air conditioner. He waited for the warm draft to transform into a cool breeze as he watched Marc entering his house and closing the door behind him.

As Phil put the car into drive, he felt relieved that he'd been able to put aside his own anger to repair his friendship. He was proud of himself, but as he drove, his thoughts wandered back to Denise. Why couldn't he have some kind of reconciliation with her like he'd just had with Marc? Every part of him wanted to try to get her back, but she had stated in the letter that if he loved her, he would respect her decision. He did still love her, so as hard as it would be to do so, he wouldn't go after her.

# Chapter 8

Phil's emotions were obviously in control, because without even meaning to, he had driven to Denise's condo. Once he realized where he was, he just allowed his car to roll right on past her property. The official ex-lover drive by—but they'd been more than lovers. They'd been friends, and that's what hurt Phil the most. That's what confused Phil the most. Friends had falling-outs all the time. Take him and Marc, for example; but true friends—real friends—they talked things out and got past it. Phil felt especially strong about that, since his chosen profession was to help people communicate better. Once his anger subsided, he knew it was only right for him to apologize to Marc for coming at him in the tone that he had. With Denise, he didn't know if he'd ever be able to go to her humbly after the way she left him. As much as he missed her, he simply refused to chase after someone who obviously felt as if he wasn't worth the race. If they were ever going to get back together, it would have to be because she reached out to him, not the other way around.

Phil glanced at Denise's place one more time in the rearview mirror before heading home. He decided that would be the last time he did that. He was not going to be prisoner to distracting feelings of regret about a situation that he couldn't change. In other words, "Fuck it. It is what it is," he told himself.

***

The following Monday, as he waited for his patient, Tina Towns, to arrive for her appointment, he went over notes he'd made the night before regarding her situation. Ironically, Tina was known as what some would call a runaway bride.

"At least she made it to the altar." Phil spoke his thoughts out loud just before Julie buzzed him, letting him know she was sending Tina in.

Phil closed Tina's casefile, pushed it aside, and pulled out pen and notebook.

"Dr. Gooden," Tina said cheerfully as she galloped into his office.

There was one thing Phil had noticed about Tina: She always looked like a blushing bride, even though commitment issues kept her from ever graduating from fiancée to actual bride.

"Hello, Tina," Phil greeted. "How are you today?"

"Fine, just fine, and happily in love." Her eyes twinkled, confirming what she had just announced, as she sat down.

"Being in love is great," Phil stated. "But this is what, your fourth engagement? I guess if anyone knows love, it's you."

"You've got that right." Tina had no problem acknowledging and admitting her truths, and the truth was, this girl had serious commitment issues.

"So, how are things with you and . . ." Phil had to quickly open his file to reference the name of fiancé number four. "Calloway?"

"Yes, Calloway," she said. "And things are better than ever." Suddenly, Tina's mile-long smile began to dissipate.

"And things being good scares you?" Phil said, jotting down notes.

"Yes. Like I told you a couple sessions ago, growing up, my siblings and I thought our parents lived the fairytale life. Never once had we ever heard them argue. They greeted and parted with a kiss. We did things together as a family. Whatever Mom wanted, Dad seemed to get it. Whatever Dad's needs were, Mom seemed to have met them." She giggled. "I know that for certain, thanks to the thin walls in the home we grew up in." Just as before, her giddy demeanor saddened.

"My mom still lives in that house, you know. She got it as part of the divorce settlement. The divorce that took place not even a month after the youngest of us kids graduated high school and left for college."

Phil handed Tina a tissue when he saw the tears forming in her eyes.

"Thank you." She dabbed her eyes dry, took a deep breath, and then continued. "None of us kids ever saw it coming. They seemed like the perfect couple. Mom was always glowing and smiling, and I thought it was because of Dad. I thought it was Dad making her so happy. My older sister and I always said that we'd marry a man like Daddy, one who could make us that happy. Come to find out, inside, Mom was as miserable as they came."

Tina paused, and Phil took that as a sign that he could speak. "Do you think your parents were ever truly happy?"

Tina thought for a moment and then shrugged. "I don't know. It's funny how things can look one way on the outside, but be something totally different on the inside."

"You've never asked your mother?"

Tina shook her head. "After the divorce, Mom was never the same. I don't know if the whole happy thing had been an act all along, or if Daddy had just broken her heart that badly by leaving her."

"So it wasn't a divorce they'd both agreed upon?" Phil questioned. "Your father left your mother?"

"Well, from what I know, he's the one who filed for the divorce, and he's the one who packed his clothes and moved out."

"From what you know? Did you not talk to your dad either?"

"Well, no. I mean, what was there to say? After seeing what he'd done to my mother, I knew I could never forgive him. He was my dad. Not only had he made my mom happy over the years, or so I thought, but he'd made us kids happy as well. He'd made me happy. So if he could hurt Mom that way, the woman who bore four children for him, then I knew he'd hurt us. I didn't want to have anything to do with him. I figured it was better to cut my ties, deal with it, and get over it, than to get hurt later."

Phil was writing, but then paused. "So are you saying that when your dad divorced your mom, you, in a sense, divorced your dad?"

Tina thought for a moment. Phil could practically see the wheels churning in her head the way her eyes shifted back and forth in thought.

"Neither you nor your siblings have a relationship with your father?" Phil asked, not seeing in her file where they'd addressed that question before.

"Well, my brother—he's the only boy—he does. My younger sister does too. My older sister and I refused. She's with me. Why set ourselves up for hurt?"

"What about your mom? Do you and all of your siblings have a relationship with your mother?"

Tina nodded. "We're all she's got. Since Dad left her, she's just lived in that house alone. Church, work, and her monthly book club meetings are her life."

"She never remarried?"

Again, Tina shook her head.

"And your father, did he ever remarry?"

"Yep, twice. His second wife died. The third wife, now, he's been married to for the past seven years. I didn't go to the wedding, but I saw some of the pictures my sister posted on Facebook." She paused. "Or was it MySpace back then? I can't remember." She let out a harrumph. "His wife looked all happy, just like Mom had been once upon a time. But let her just wait and see. He'll probably leave her hurt, bitter, and depressed the same way he left Mom. Probably would have done that to his last wife as well if she hadn't died. Heck, she was lucky. She got out of the marriage before he could hurt her. I don't know what I would do if that happened to me. . . ." Her words trailed off.

Phil gave her a minute to allow her to finish her thoughts. "You have to go talk to your father, Tina. Find out his side of the story. There are three sides to what happened between your parents: hers, his, and the truth. You need to talk through this with both of them. Separately, I would guess. Heaven forbid, what if something happened to one or both of them and you were still holding onto this grudge? It would break your heart."

Tina looked down at the floor. Phil could tell that he had gotten to her. He knew that even if she didn't change completely, something was going to be different after that conversation.

"You are still your daddy's little girl. Talk to him."

Tina's eyes darted to and locked with Phil's. She looked as though she'd been keeping a secret and had now been found out. At the same time, behind her eyes was a little glimmer, reflecting that she didn't mind being discovered. As tears spilled out and her bottom lip began to tremble, Phil knew that this was becoming a bit too overwhelming for his patient. Still, he was glad to have found what he believed to be the source of Tina's perpetual cold feet.

"Why don't we stop here, let you catch your breath, and then pick things up at your next visit?

"Okay. I think that's a good idea."

"But I want you to really think about what I said."

Tina sniffed and nodded. Phil gave her a moment to gather herself. Finally she grabbed her purse and stood. "Thank you," she managed to get out before she started to tear up again.

Phil allowed her this moment. This had been a breakthrough of some kind. Tina had always presented herself as a bubbly and upbeat person and had never shown anywhere near this much emotional depth. She had years of tears, grief, and heartache to release. He did not want to rush this healing process and risk Calloway becoming jilted groom number four. More importantly, he didn't want to scare her away before she opened up to allow herself the true love she deserved.

Once Tina left Phil's office, he walked over to the window and gazed outside. He felt confident that he'd reached the core of Tina's issues, and as he replayed some of their previous conversations in his mind, a lightbulb went off in his head.

He raced back over to his desk and opened Tina's file, flipping through papers that contained notes of their sessions. Each time Tina had run off on one of her fiancés, she'd left a note. Those notes explained her true feelings, but they were just the surface of her feelings. What she'd revealed today was the underbelly.

Phil flipped to page he'd been looking for and scanned it. He read over something he'd written down that Tina had said. Putting the paper down on the desk, he repeated her words out loud. "None of them ever came for me."

Not one of the three men Tina had left at the altar ever went back for her. Phil could imagine the hurt, embarrassment, and devastation each of the men might have felt, but every last one of them took the words in her letter at face value and left it at that. What if just one of them had gone after her, fought for her, forcing her to dig deep and unpeel the layers that existed within? They would have known that it wasn't them she was running from; it was her own life.

Feeling momentarily inspired, he pulled out his phone, thinking he would not make the same mistakes as Tina's fiancés, but almost as quickly as it had come over him, that feeling of determination was gone. Just as he understood that Tina had wanted the men to fight for her, he also understood that the men were too hurt, and probably embarrassed, to do that. A man would have to be totally willing to set aside his ego to go after a woman who had already rejected him, and Phil didn't know if he was willing to do that. After all, Denise wasn't making any effort to reach out to him. How was it supposed to work if only one person was willing to fight for what they had? He put away his cell phone without making the call.

The blinking light on his office phone alerted him that he had voice mail waiting, so he pressed the button to listen to the messages. There was only one, and it was from Mr. Adams, the bitter, quiet man forced to attend the therapy sessions. He had left Phil a message, wanting to confirm that Phil would be handling his case from now on. He also wanted to know when they could continue that chess game. Phil listened to the message with a smile on his face. The man who wouldn't say anything at first was now calling him and requesting another session.

If Mr. Adams was coming back, Phil knew that he was going to have to freshen up his jazz playlist, and he didn't mind doing so. If music and chess were going to help Mr. Adams continue to open up, then it was well worth it.

Phil logged in to his computer and opened up iTunes, but before he could start searching for new jazz to download, Julie hurried through the door without knocking.

"Wow! What did you do to her?"

"What do you mean?" he asked, confused.

"She's out there on the phone crying tears of joy." Julie moved to the side and pointed toward the doorway.

Phil looked into the waiting area to see Tina pacing in a small circle as she engaged in a phone conversation. She was using all kinds of hand gestures, and she looked to be smiling, crying, and laughing.

"I think she's talking to her father. I heard her say 'I miss you Daddy,'" Julie surmised. "She was giving you all kinds of praises, saying she never would have made the call if it wasn't for you."

Phil exhaled; it was laced with a sigh.

"What? You don't seem too thrilled," Julie said. "I was coming in here to give you kudos. Good work, Doctor Gooden. Looks like another success story. Thought that would make you happy."

"And it does make me happy," Phil said. Because of him, a woman's relationship with her father was on the road to mending. He allowed a smile to take over his face.

"So why don't we go celebrate? It's my lunch hour, and you don't have a client for another hour and a half."

Phil thought for a moment. *Food*. When was the last time he'd had a decent meal, or even ate, for that matter? It had been almost three weeks since Denise had left him. He'd been running non-stop, keeping himself busy in order to keep his mind off of Denise.

"Come on, I'll buy," Julie pressed, batting her eyes and pouting her lips like a sad little puppy dog. She folded her arms. "And I'm not leaving this office until you say yes."

He looked at Julie. On cue, his stomach growled. Good company and good food, both something he'd been lacking. Plus, he didn't want to disappoint Julie. Here she was trying to do something nice for him.

Phil grabbed his suit jacket and walked over to Julie with his elbow extended. A huge smile spread across Julie's face as she looped her arm through his.

*A quick meal couldn't hurt,* Phil thought to himself. *Or could it?*

# Chapter 9

"Oh, is that how you two gon' play me?" Marc shouted out when he saw Julie and Phil heading out of the lobby arm in arm.

"We're just headed to lunch," Julie said to him.

"Well, hell, I'm hungry too." Marc rubbed his stomach.

"Your next clients, Mr. and Mrs. Walker, should be here any minute."

"Guess that means we'll have to bring you something back," Phil teased.

"Oh, man, you wrong for that," Marc whined as if his best friend was stealing the girl he'd had his eyes on. That wasn't too far from the truth. Marc had been trying to get with Julie. Then again, what woman hadn't Marc been known to try to get with? "You ain't been broken up with Denise but three weeks," Marc shouted out to his best friend, "and now you trying to steal my girl." Marc gave Julie a supposedly seductive look that left her totally uninspired.

There was a sudden awkward silence that filled the space. Julie looked at Phil, surprised; Phil looked at Marc, pissed, and Marc looked at Phil with regret. Marc could tell by the way Phil was staring at him that Julie hadn't been privy to the beans he'd just spilled.

Marc looked down at his watch. "Oooh, look at that. Mr. and Mrs. Walker will be here any minute. I better go look over their casefile before they arrive." He turned and hurried into his office, not even waiting for Julie or Phil to respond. He could feel his best friend's eyes burning through him. He knew he'd hear all about it later.

Marc went into his office and sat down. Mr. and Mrs. Walker's casefile was the last thing on his mind. Checking his Facebook newsfeed was the first. He'd managed to update his status, like a few sexy photos of some of his female Facebook friends, and comment on a couple of things in the newsfeed before his clients came in and he started their session.

As usual, Mr. and Mrs. Walker hadn't been in there ten minutes before they started going in on each other. Marc sat at his desk, looking distraught as they bickered back and forth. He let them go at for a while as he posted a picture on Instagram and responded to a direct message. Finally, their fussing was starting to escalate.

"I can't stand you!" Mr. Walker shouted at his wife.

"I can't stand you either," Mrs. Walker returned with a head wobble.

"I'm just waiting for the day that they legalize marital abuse, 'cause I'ma smack a shade of black off of your ass," he threatened.

"Do it, and that will be the day that you die."

Although Marc could have gone all day listening to these two fuss like Fred Sanford and Aunt Esther, he knew he had to calm them down before their yelling carried out into the waiting room. The last thing he needed was for Phil to come back from lunch and hear that kind of racket.

"Why are you two still married?" he interrupted them.

Mrs. Walker paused, turning her attention from fussing out her husband to her therapist. "Excuse me?" she said with a little sista-tude.

"I said why are you two still together? Why don't you just get a divorce so you can stop getting on each other's nerves and you can stop getting on mine?"

Mr. Walker jumped up out of his seat. "Wait a minute! Nobody talks to my wife like that."

Mrs. Walker stood next to him. "That's right. You tell him, baby." She looped her arm through her husband's. That was the most intimacy Marc had ever witnessed between them.

Marc allowed his eyes to travel from one to the other. "Something is definitely wrong with both of you. And look at that." Marc tapped his watch. "Your time is up, so this session is over."

The couple shot each other puzzled looks.

Mr. Walker turned his attention back to Marc. "Hold up. We just got here."

"Yeah, and I thought you were supposed to help us fix our issues," Mrs. Walker chimed in.

The couple had finally agreed on something and were on the same side. That still didn't make Marc change his mind about not wanting to continue with their session. He had a headache.

"What's there to fix?" Marc asked the couple. "You two are perfect for each other. You're both crazy as hell."

Mr. Walker pulled his wife tightly against him and escorted her to the door. "We don't have to take this."

Marc walked over to the door with them. "You sure don't. Here's the hallway." He ushered the couple out and then closed the door behind them. "They don't pay me enough for this," he mumbled as he walked back over to his desk.

He picked up his phone and noticed that he had a missed call and a voice message. As he connected to his voice mail and listened to the message, he rushed to grab a pen and something to write on. The nearest thing was one of his client's casefiles. He opened it up and began scribbling down information from the voice message that included a date, time, and address. He'd transfer it over to his calendar as soon as he got a chance.

Right after he deleted the message, his phone vibrated. He had another call coming in.

"Hello?" He answered and listened for a second to the caller. "As a matter of fact, I just got the message," he said.

While the caller talked, Marc scrambled around in his briefcase in an attempt to locate his calendar. He turned to the current month then said, "That's a Monday." He frowned. "I usually don't—" The caller cut him off, and as Marc listened, his eyes grew wide.

"Say no more. I'm there." He ended the call and penned in the information he'd written in the casefile onto his calendar.

If his body hadn't been still aching from his game of one on one with Phil the other day, he would have jumped up and kicked his heels. This phone call was just what he needed right now. It was the break he needed. If everything panned out as he hoped, he could get back to focusing on his job one hundred percent.

"Ahhh, who am I kidding?" he said out loud, waving his hand dismissively in the air. "Maybe seventy percent, even eighty for my boy's sake, but never one hundred percent," he told himself.

Even without life's current distractions, Marc had never been as serious about this whole therapy thing as Phil had been, but that was okay with him. It was important to him to always have someone in his circle who was better than him at something, or at several things. That way, he would be constantly inspired to strive for more. Phil fit that bill perfectly; he was more successful, smarter, and definitely better off financially. Marc genuinely wanted to be more like the man that Phil was, but he had to admit that most times he didn't follow through and make any moves forward.

He wasn't beating himself up or looking down on himself, though. Being honest with himself was something Marc was good at. Being honest with everybody else was a whole other story.

"I don't know for the life of me how you can work with him, let alone hang out with him after work," Julie said, squinting up her face.

"Aww, he's not that bad," Phil said, taking a bite of his grilled chicken sandwich.

"Ha! Lies," Julie said, taking a sip of her cherry Coke. "But you just go ahead and keep lying to yourself. I know the truth about why you keep him around." Julie puckered her lips and winked.

"Woman, what are you talking about?" Phil asked with a slight chuckle.

"He makes you look good." She shrugged her shoulders. "Not that you don't already look good." She gave him a playful once-over. "But he makes you look better. Trust me, I know all about it. Mean girls used to do that back in school all the time. They'd befriend the little ol' homely-looking girl so that they would look just that much finer standing next to the poor thing."

Phil burst out laughing. "That's crazy. And you're right about one thing: that's only something a mean person would do, and I'm not mean. I'm . . ." Phil tried to think of the right words to describe himself. "Just me. And you couldn't be more wrong. I keep him around because I want to see him win, like a real friend does, and I know the potential he has."

"I guess you are a real gem, Dr. Gooden," Julie said in a playfully sarcastic tone.

"So what's your problem, Julie? Why are you single?" Phil asked, pointing a fry at her.

"Whoa, hold up. Wait a minute," Julie said, snapping her neck back and holding up her hands. "Being single is not the plague. What makes men think some of us don't want to be single?" Julie was stern, holding her ground with her head held high and shoulders up.

"Because you don't. Yes, you may dress up for yourself, get made up and make sure your hair is on point for yourself, but at the end of the day, part of you is hoping that the right man, someone truly worthy of your time, will see you for the amazing woman that you are."

Julie looked at Phil in shock, as if he had just read her mind.

Phil took a look at Julie. It was obvious that she wasn't originally from California. It was good to see that she was okay with whatever God had blessed her with. She hadn't gotten into some of the cosmetic alterations some L.A. women had.

For some strange reason, thoughts of Julie brought on thoughts of Denise, and how the two women truly were opposites in so many areas. Denise was a personal stylist for celebrities. That was a part of her life, so every now and then she'd indulge. Nothing major, just a Botox party here and there and the occasional waist-trainer. Image had been so important to her, but he had never really noticed until now.

"Everything okay?"

Julie's inquiry broke Phil from his thoughts.

"Oh, yeah, yeah, I'm good." He picked up his sandwich to take a bite. Realizing he'd lost his appetite, he put it back down.

"Is it her? Denise?" Julie asked. She thought back to the slip-up comment Marc had made back at the office. Since Phil hadn't elaborated on it during their trip to the café, Julie hadn't asked. Now, seeing how his entire demeanor had shifted, she felt led to ask.

Phil looked into Julie's eyes. Wasn't it like dating 101 for a man not to discuss his relationship woes with another woman? But then again, Julie wasn't just some other woman. She was his friend and coworker—and this wasn't really a date, was it? On top of all of that, technically there was no longer a relationship between him and Denise.

"Yeah, I try not to think about her, but I can't help it."

"How long have you two been broken up?" Julie asked. "I thought I just saw her at the office not too long ago."

"You did," Phil assured her. "A few weeks ago, and that was the last time I saw her too. Right after I proposed to her."

"Oh, no." Julie gasped, covering her mouth with her hands. "She didn't accept your proposal? I can only imagine."

"Oh, she accepted the proposal," Phil said. "I couldn't wait to get home and start sharing wedding ideas."

"Oh, yeah," Julie recalled. "In your work boots. I remember."

Phil cleared his throat, smirked a little, and continued on without addressing Julie's last comment. "But once I got home, I found the ring and a letter from Denise saying that she just wasn't ready."

"Ouch," Julie said. "A letter, huh?"

Phil nodded.

"Well, look at the bright side. At least it wasn't a text."

He didn't even crack a smile.

Julie shrugged. "I was just saying. It could be worse."

"I know. You were just trying to help." Phil turned and raised his hand, signaling the waitress to come to their table. He wasn't really in the mood to talk about all that.

"I'm sorry. I was just trying to—"

"No need to apologize, Julie. I know you meant well," Phil said, cutting her off. Lunch had been going well. Spending time with Julie had been a pleasant change in his mood, but then he had to go and start talking about Denise. He should have just gone with his first instinct and deflected her question.

The perky waitress came over to the table and asked, "Is there anything else I can get for you guys?"

"Just the check please," Phil said.

The waitress looked at their plates. They each had at least half of their meals left. "No problem. I'll grab you a couple of to-go boxes as well," she said then headed off.

"Well, thanks for lunch," Phil said, not allowing time for awkward silence.

"It was my pleasure," Julie said.

"Next time lunch is on me." Phil knew he'd ruined lunch with his talk about Denise. He'd make it up to Julie when he was in a better mood.

"Sounds good. I'm going to hold you to that."

The waitress returned with the check and the boxes. She went to give the check to Phil, but Julie was quick to let her know that she'd be taking care of the tab.

After paying the bill, with to-go boxes in hand, Julie and Phil exited the restaurant. Phil realized that this little lunch and Marc's big mouth could possibly have made things really messy around the office. He would just have to wait and see.

# Chapter 10

"So when you gon' let me take you out to lunch?" Marc asked, standing over Julie's desk.

"Not hungry," Julie said, not even looking up from her computer at Marc.

Marc sucked his teeth. "I'm not talking about today. I know you had lunch with my boy earlier today. But there's always dinner, and it is just about dinner time." Marc leaned down over Julie's shoulder. "Or we could just skip dinner and get right down to dessert."

Julie shivered at Marc's hot breath burning down her neck. She jerked away from him and whipped around to face him. "Do you mind getting out of my space?"

"Oh, she's a feisty one." Marc backed up, raising his hands in defense. "I like that in a woman. A lioness." He let out a little roaring sound. "What are you, a Leo? Mm-hmm. And I bet you like to get wild."

"You can't be serious right now. To think that it's okay to just hound a woman like this. I mean, does that actually get you dates?" Julie didn't wait for Marc to answer. "No, it couldn't possibly." She shook her head. "Because I've never seen you with a woman. Nope, not once. Never seen you take a woman out to lunch."

He leaned down and rubbed Julie's chin with his index finger. "But you, I would. You are a beautiful, classy, intellectually stimulating lady."

Julie pulled her face away. "Well, like I said, I'm not hungry. I got plenty full with Phil today." Julie purposely said that last comment with a hint of seduction. Maybe if Marc thought she was trying to get with his best friend, he'd lay off, although knowing Marc, he'd want to have a threesome. If that didn't work, he'd settle to simply watch.

"Oh, so you after my boy? I tried to tell him." Marc smiled knowingly.

Julie wasn't smiling. She was horrified. "You tried to tell him what?" She stood up abruptly from her desk.

"Oh, and I see the lioness has claws as well." Marc pretended his hands were a lion's paws and teasingly clawed at Julie.

She shook her head, getting more aggravated by the moment with this character before her. "You know what? Just forget it. I don't even know why I entertain you." She sat back down in her chair just as Phil's door opened.

"Speak of the devil," Marc said, glancing from Phil then to Julie, giving her a devilish look. "We were just talking about you, Dr. Gooden. Weren't we, Miss Julie?"

Julie rolled her eyes up in her head, let out an "Ugh," and then turned her attention back to her computer.

It didn't take a rocket scientist to see that Julie was more than annoyed by Marc. Phil figured Marc had been out there doing his flirting thing. He'd told Julie he would talk to Marc about that, which he hadn't yet. There was no better time than the present, he decided.

"Can I talk to you in your office for a second?" Phil asked Marc.

"Sure. What's up?" Marc asked nervously. As of late, any talk with Phil hadn't been about anything good.

"We'll talk in your office," Phil said, putting his arm around Marc's shoulder and escorting him into his own office.

Phil closed the door behind them. "So what's up with Julie?" he asked. "She seemed a bit bothered."

Marc sat on the edge of his desk. "Oh, that. She's just tripping." He waved his hand, downplaying it. "You know how them chicks be trying to act. I was just complimenting her and she got all uptight."

"Then maybe you shouldn't compliment her anymore," Phil said sternly.

Marc pulled his upper body back and glared at his best friend. "Wait a minute. So now that you and Denise are no longer an item, you gon' try to . . . You want to get with—Ohhhh, I see." He shot Phil a mischievous look and began to nod. He stood up and held his hands up. "Okay, brotha. You don't have to tell me twice. Hey, I'll back off if you want to get with ol' girl."

Phil had to stare at his friend for a moment to see if he was serious. Of course he was serious. This was Marc he was talking about. "I can't with you." Phil shook his head. "I don't want Julie romantically. We're just friends. It was a celebratory lunch. But still, lay off of her. She's not interested, as you could clearly see. Move on to your next victim—I mean target."

Marc glared at Phil, who added, "But just make sure none of them work here at the office."

"I hear you. I'll lay off Julie since you done called bingo on her."

"Man, I said I don't want Julie."

"You just don't want me to have her, huh?"

Phil shook his head. He wasn't going to keep going back and forth with Marc. He was already starting to get a headache. "Look, this is your boss talking. Your flirting makes her uncomfortable, so stop it, period. End of discussion. I have to work to get back to, and I'm certain you do too."

"*Pshtt.* You're just bound and determined to stay busy," Marc said. "That's all you've been doing lately is keeping your face buried in them casefiles. That's not going to change the fact that she's gone. You're going to have to deal with it at some point."

"Anyway," Phil said, ignoring Marc's advice and changing the subject in a hurry, "don't forget we're watching the game at your house on Thursday, and let Herb know he better not forget to bring beer. He been drinking up everybody else's for the last two games."

Phil and Marc, along with a couple of the dudes they sometimes balled with on Saturdays, took turns hosting the games at their homes. This time it was Marc's turn. At first Marc used to find all kinds of excuses why he shouldn't host, but now that he had his new top of the line living room set, there was no shame in his game.

Even though Marc had never admitted it, Phil knew that one of the reasons Marc had gone out and put himself in such debt for the expensive furniture was because of the game get-togethers. Out of all the fellas, Marc's place was the least decorative, for lack of a better term. Phil had watched the expression on Marc's face when he'd go to the other guys' homes. Then he'd listen to Marc make excuses about his own home.

"Pardon the house, fellas. A brother is in the process of redecorating," he'd said with a nervous chuckle, while tossing ripped pillows behind the couch.

Phil knew Marc and could see right through his act. Besides, he'd never mentioned anything to him about redecorating. His old couch had seemed to do just fine until he saw how everyone else was living and decided he needed to keep up with the Joneses.

"All right," Marc said. "Game day, my house. I got you."

"Later." Phil exited Marc's office and headed back toward his own. He stopped at Julie's desk to touch base with her.

"You good?" Phil asked Julie, who was still looking a little touched after her encounter with Marc.

She shot Phil an irritated look. "I love working here, I swear to God I do, but if I have to continue to deal with Dr. Collins, then—"

"You won't." Phil cut her off. "I just talked to Dr. Collins about all his flirting and coming on to you. Just like I told you I would."

Julie looked at Phil doubtfully as she turned off her computer.

"I promise I did. I wouldn't play around with something like that."

Phil was pretty certain that Julie wouldn't take it to the next level now that she'd complained about Marc's unwanted advances, but he knew he had a legal obligation to act on her complaint. As her employer, he had to do something about it or she could end up suing the entire company. He wanted to make sure she understood that he had taken her complaint seriously. "You won't be having any more problems out of him. If you do, let me know."

A light smile parted Julie's lips. She really did have a nice smile.

"Well, thank you, Phil. I appreciate it." She turned off the lamp on her desk.

Phil looked down at his watch. "I can't believe it's that time already."

"Yep, it's closing time," Julie said. "For me anyway. I notice you've been staying late."

"Well, not tonight. Let me grab my things real quick. I'll give you a ride."

Julie put her hand up to decline, but Phil had already darted off to his office. Julie took the next minute or so to finish gathering her things and get her desk ready for the next day.

"You all set?" Phil asked, coming out of his office with his briefcase in hand.

"I don't need a ride," Julie told him. "You live in the total opposite direction."

Phil shrugged. "It's cool. It's only about twenty minutes out of the way."

"In L.A. traffic?" Julie laughed.

"Yeah, you are right. But still. It's not a problem."

"My ride should be here shortly. Thanks for the offer though."

"Are you sure?"

Julie put her hands on her hips "Yes, I'm sure. And why are you offering me a ride now?"

"I just noticed that you've been getting dropped off lately. At least let me walk you out. There are some crazy folks in L.A. It ain't always safe for a lady like yourself."

"I think I'm safer out there than in here." She rolled her eyes toward Marc's office.

"I told you I took care of that. He's going to lay off of you."

"And I appreciate that very much," Julie said. She grabbed her purse off her desk. "By the way, just what did you say to get him to agree to lay off flirting with me?"

"It was simple," Phil said with a shrug. "I told him to back up because I wanted you."

The look on Julie's face was priceless. Her eyes bucked and her cheeks turned red. She was the prettiest shade of chocolate, so getting her to blush took some doing.

"I'm just kidding," Phil said with a smile.

It took a couple seconds, but ultimately Julie started laughing too. It was a light chuckle at first, but then it was a full blown laugh. "I knew you were just joking." She playfully hit Phil on the arm. "Boy, you are so crazy. Just funny. Whew, you crack me up." Julie took off walking ahead of Phil after her fake laugh ceased.

"Yeah, I am crazy, aren't I?" Phil asked, standing there for a minute. He'd be crazy not to have seen the momentary beam of hope in Julie's eyes when he'd told her what he said to Marc. He would have been crazy not to have seen that hope evaporate into hopelessness. He and Julie definitely had chemistry. She was a beautiful, smart, and sophisticated woman. Any brother would be blessed to have her as his woman. Was he passing up a blessing? He knew for sure that plenty of brothers would call him crazy for not acting on the chemistry between them. After all, who passes up a woman like that?

"You coming or what?" Julie said to Phil while she waited for him at the door.

He snapped out of his thoughts and locked eyes with her. "Yes, I'm coming." He walked to the lobby and held open the door for Julie to exit.

"Thank you, kind sir." Julie did a curtsy as she walked out of the building.

Phil watched her gorgeous figure strut across the parking lot like it was a runway. A little voice in his head urged him to take a chance. They had synergy, a palpable connection between them, one that was more powerful than Phil was ready to acknowledge just yet. "It's too soon," Phil reminded himself as he turned and walked in the other direction. "Too soon."

# Chapter 11

Julie knocked on Marc's office door and peeked into his office. "Dr. Collins, your four o'clock appointment just called. She said she's parking and will be up in a minute. Do you want me to send her right in?"

Marc looked up from his *Hip Hop Weekly* magazine. His feet were kicked up on his desk. "Intercom still broken, Julie?"

"Yes. I'll call them again." Julie had already called maintenance about the intercom earlier that morning when they'd realized the system wasn't working.

"Thank you. Send her on in when she gets up here, please," Marc said as he continued to flip through the pages. A couple seconds later, realizing Julie was still in the doorway, Marc looked up. "Is there something else?"

"Oh, no, no. That's it," Julie said. She slowly exited the office, surprised that Marc hadn't tried to hit on her or said one inappropriate thing to her. She smiled, glad Phil's little talk with Marc had actually worked.

Once Marc's patient showed up, Julie showed her right into his office and went back to her desk to start finishing up for the day. Phil came out to the lobby at quarter after five. Even though Julie was off the clock at five, she was never in any rush to leave, unlike Marc. He was often the last one to get there and the first to leave.

"Is Marc still in his session?" Phil asked. Typically Marc would swing by Phil's office to say good-bye—at 4:59 p.m.

"Yep," Julie said.

Phil looked over at Marc's door. "Who's he in with?"

"Janell Andrews. She's a new patient. Pretty young girl. This is only her second session, I believe."

A suspicious look covered Phil's face as he continued to stare at the door. He thought out loud. "I wonder if she's that good-looking college student he was telling me about." Phil surely couldn't fathom Marc staying late for any other reason. He was allergic to going above and beyond.

Julie thought for a second. "Yep, that would probably be her." She finished gathering up her things. She wasn't the least bit concerned. Hell, anything to keep Marc from bothering her.

Phil made his way over to Marc's door. He knocked, but there was no answer. There wasn't any talking either. He heard some rustling around. "Dr. Collins," Phil called out. Once again, he got no response, but he could clearly hear someone inside the office. He checked the doorknob, but it was locked. He knocked again, slightly harder this time. "Dr. Collins, I need to see you out here, please."

Finally Marc came out of the office, quickly closing the door behind him. He was breathing hard, sweating slightly, and he was straightening his clothes and tucking his shirt inside his pants.

Phil tried to look over Marc's shoulder and into the office before the door had closed behind him, to no avail. "Is that your four o'clock appointment still in there?"

"Uh, yes, sir," Marc said, trying to sound professional. "We were wrestling with some serious issues in there today." He cleared his throat. "But we're starting to get to the bottom of it."

"I bet you are." Phil gave Marc a sermon with just a look, and Marc heard every word of it. Whether it would make any difference would remain to be seen.

"Well, uh, I need to get back on top of this situation. We'll talk later." Marc rushed back in his office, quickly closing the door behind him.

Phil stood there with the door closed in his face. "Some things never change." He turned to see Julie standing there, having watched the whole scene go down. "And aren't you supposed to be gone already?"

"Waiting on my ride," Julie said with a blushing smile.

"All right, then. Got a little glow going on."

Julie didn't respond as she switched away to the exit, a smile still on her face.

"Well, you be safe."

"I always am." Julie turned around and winked, then pushed the door open and left.

"Enjoy your ride," Phil said, even though Julie was long gone and couldn't hear him. Suddenly, an emotion hit him that caught him off guard and threw him for a loop—jealousy.

# Chapter 12

"You know you gotta stop, right?" Phil asked Marc as he bent over the pool table with stick in hand, preparing to make his shot. After watching the game at Marc's house, the fellas decided to go shoot some pool at the sports bar around the corner.

"I know." Marc hated to admit it.

Phil looked over at his best friend. "No, for real, man."

"I hear you," Marc said, then under his breath mumbled, "Like you ain't never done it."

"I haven't," Phil said. "Now, Denise got it a few times at the office, but I've never slept with a patient."

"TMI. I don't need to hear anymore. I'll stop, for real," Marc said. "But I don't wanna hear nothing if you catch me and one of my girls messing around at the office."

"I won't say a word, as long as she's not a patient. For all I care, you can put her on your desk. It's sturdy enough." Phil bent down again to take his shot.

Marc watched curiously as a question popped in his head. "Wait. How do you know that my desk is sturdy enough to . . ."

Phil gave Marc a mischievous look and then took his shot.

Marc scrunched his face up. "You and Denise . . . on my desk . . . I eat off that desk!"

Even though Phil had missed his shot, he stood up with a proud look on his face. "Me too," he said. "Me too."

"You so wrong, man." Marc shook his head. "That's why you missed your shot." Marc leaned in to take his own shot, which landed in the pocket. He stood up as tall as his big ego required him to. "You owe me ten bucks, loser."

"So what." Phil shrugged. "I still had sex on your desk. And I better not catch you on mine with anyone."

The two men shared a laugh as they prepared for another game of pool. Phil reached in his pocket and laid a twenty-dollar bill on the pool table.

"Oh, so we betting twenty instead of the usual ten?" Marc questioned as he chalked his pool stick. "Guess you mad I just won your money. You trying to win your ten back plus make a come-up?" Marc asked.

"Man, just put your money up," Phil snapped. His attitude revealed that Marc was right in his assumption.

Phil and Marc played their game, and Phil won the second one. They played until they lost count of the number of games that had gone by, like they always did. Afterward, they sat at the bar, watching some college hoop and talking.

"I don't know how regular people do it," Phil said.

"Regular people?" Marc questioned, taking a sip of his beer. "What do you mean?"

"I've studied the mind. I've treated the mind. I know how to take control of it when it wants to run wild. I know better. I can weigh the consequences." Phil took a sip of his Hennessey. He frowned as it burned down his throat. Once his throat had cooled down, he spoke. "Never thought I'd find myself in the same position as some of my clients."

"Yeah, well, like you said," Marc reasoned as he sipped from his beer bottle, "life happens—to regular folks and to us." Marc's mind seemed to wander off to a personal space.

Phil sensed in Marc's voice that his mind was consumed with issues of his own. "You good over there, man?" He elbowed Marc.

"Huh? Yeah." Marc snapped out of his daze. He cleared his throat. "So, uh, still no word from Denise?"

Phil shook his head.

"You thought about calling her?"

"Ha! Have I?" Phil said. "I was this close to calling her the other day." He held a small space between his thumb and index finger. "And I even . . ." Phil's words trailed off as he thought about whether he wanted to continue. He looked at Marc, who didn't seem to be in one of his jokey-jokey moods. Perhaps he could vent without being hit by one of his smartass comments. He took his chances. "I even drove to her condo Saturday after I left your place."

Marc turned and looked at him with surprise. "For real? Well, what did she say?" He turned in his chair, ready to get the 411.

Phil shook his head. "I didn't go in."

Marc turned back to the bar. "I don't blame you. I mean, what is there to say? If somebody don't want you, then they just don't want you."

"Wow. That makes me feel better."

"Oh, my bad. I didn't mean it like that. Nothing's wrong with being alone. Society makes us think we always gotta be booed up or shackled to someone. Committed."

"But I love women. The black woman is just everything," Phil said.

"I didn't say be celibate or no crazy stuff like that," Marc clarified. "I'm just saying, having fun. Get you a couple friends." Marc took another sip of his beer. "With benefits."

"That's just not who I am. You know that," Phil said.

"Then try being something different," Marc suggested. As he finished off his beer, he got an idea. "You know that nurse I be hooking up with sometimes?"

Phil thought for a minute. "The real nurse, or the one who dresses up like a nurse?"

Marc laughed. "The real one. Shayla. The one I introduced to you that time at the restaurant."

"Oh, yeah, the time you didn't have enough money to cover y'all's tab and you needed me to come bail you out," Phil said. He'd had to loan Marc almost a hundred dollars to cover the bill.

"Yeah, that one." Marc exhaled, hating to be reminded of the incident. "I didn't know she was going to order the highest thing on the menu. I don't know what a brother would have done if you hadn't come through. Her bedroom skills are bananas, and I know I wouldn't have gotten any that night if she had to pay for own her meal."

"You're sick," Phil said.

"I'm just glad I was able to call you to come help me out."

"Yeah, faking like I just happened to be in the restaurant and you ran into me." Phil shook his head. "I'd rather be by myself than go through all those shenanigans. The whole dating thing is just too much. Takes up too much time and too much damn effort."

"You don't know that. You haven't dated in years," Marc said. "So I was thinkiiiiiing . . ."

From the way Marc's words got all sing-song and trailed off, Phil knew this wasn't going to be good. The mere fact that Marc was thinking was never good.

"I'm getting with Shayla this weekend, and she has a friend, actually a couple hot friends—"

"Oh, no." Phil put his hands up and shook them, refusing Marc's suggestion before he could even get it all the way out.

Marc just talked loudly over him. "I think you would hit it off really well with one of them."

"Nope, no, and hell no," Phil said, shaking his head adamantly.

"Come on. You need to get out. Get your mind off things," Marc insisted.

Phil's mind was not going to be changed. He'd never been on a blind date in his life, and he wasn't going to start now.

"Okay, then just come hang out with me and Shayla. She's gonna cook us up something to eat and we're going to hang out. You do know what 'hang out' means, right?"

"I know what it is. I mean, do you even get through dinner before pouncing on the chick?" Phil laughed.

"Shayla isn't that kind of girl," Marc said, genuinely feeling a little offended.

"Not that kind of girl? You just said the chick was a freak."

"Yeah, but she's different. I like this one, so it's not always about getting some with her. Just most of the time," Marc said with a laugh.

Phil shot Marc a disapproving glance.

"Come on, man. Shayla's a good girl. Like I said, just come hang out with her. She's cool people, and so are her friends. Then maybe you'll let me set you up with one."

Phil did entertain the thought for a moment. It wouldn't hurt to get out of the house and do something. Besides that, what was the harm in just hanging out with Marc and Shayla?

"What the hell." Phil gave in.

"Yes! That's my boy. That's the Phil I used to know before he got all whipped. Now a brotha trying to act like he ain't never love 'em and leave 'em."

"I said I'd hang out with you and Shayla. That's it. And for the record, I've never been as bad as you! Remember, I was the guy you teased for being a serial monogamist," Phil clarified. "The fact that I'm actually going to show up is saying a lot."

"Okay, okay. This is a start." Marc backed off, just glad Phil was even willing to do that much. Usually once his mind was made up, there was no changing it. "So be at my house Friday at around eight," Marc told Phil.

"I'll be there." Phil stood. "But right now I need to get my ass home before I show up at work tomorrow looking like you."

"Forget you, man," Marc said, standing as well. "I been looking good this week. Been on my A game."

"It's only Tuesday," Phil reminded him. "But you were clean today. I'll give you that."

Phil threw Marc a peace sign then strolled off into the night like President Obama. When he got in his car, he started it but didn't pull off immediately. He sat there momentarily, thoughts of Denise once again trying to invade his head space. He hated feeling this way. It felt so foreign to him. He hated to admit it, but maybe Marc was right. Maybe it was time for him to put himself back out there. Who was to say it was too soon? Love don't wait on nobody.

He started his car, now more willing than before to meet with Shayla and see about connecting with one of her girlfriends. After all, it was worth a try . . . maybe.

# Chapter 13

Phil arrived at Marc's house at eight o'clock on the nose. Even though Marc had told him that he didn't need to bring anything, Phil's mother had taught him it was poor etiquette to arrive at someone's house for an event empty handed, so Phil had stopped and picked up a veggie tray and a bottle of white wine. When he got to Marc's doorstep, the large front door was open, so it was just the screen door separating him from the inside. Typically he would have just walked right in, but he thought better of it. Leave it to Marc to try to be doing something freaky with his new girlfriend when Phil walked in. That was the last thing he wanted to witness, so Phil opted to ring the bell.

"Come on in," he heard Marc call out.

When Phil opened the door, Marc was sitting on the couch with his arm wrapped around a brown-skinned woman. Shayla had long, curly hair that looked to be mostly hers, and a nice smile.

"Everybody decent?" Phil teased as he stepped inside.

"What's up, man?" Marc removed his arm from around the woman and stood to give Phil a pound.

"Nothing too much," Phil answered. "Just winding down for the weekend. Going to try not to work and just relax. It's nice to see you again," Phil said to Shayla.

She stood and extended her hand to greet Phil.

Shayla let out a soft laugh. "It's very nice to see you again as well, Phil. I know we really didn't get to talk in

the restaurant, but I've heard a lot about you from Marc."
She straightened out her denim skirt as she sat back
down. "All good things."

Marc chimed in after taking the lid off the container of
veggies. "Yeah, and I take them all back." He laughed as
he sat down on the couch next to Shayla.

"If I recall correctly," Phil said, "I crashed your first
date with Marc."

Shayla smiled and turned to face Marc. "Yes, that was
our first date."

It didn't go unnoticed by Phil how Shayla's eyes lit up
at the mere mention of Marc's name. It was how Denise's
eyes used to light up whenever she gazed into his. Phil
stopped his mind from wandering to thoughts of Denise,
because this night was not supposed to be about her. In
fact, it was supposed to be about him getting his mind off
of her.

Shayla went back into the kitchen to tend to the food.

"You'll never guess who I saw today," Marc said in
a low tone, trying to keep the conversation from being
heard by Shayla.

"Who?" Phil asked, intrigued.

"Denise."

In spite of his desire to keep his mind off of her, Phil
perked up when he heard her name. "Where'd you see
her?"

"CityWalk. I was eating lunch and I saw her walk past
with some big six foot nine cat. Must have been one of
them ball-playing guys."

This news hit Phil hard, but unfortunately, it hadn't
come as a total surprise. If he was being honest with
himself, Denise had always been about appearances,
labels, and material things. She had also been complaining for the last couple of months about having to work.
One time, she went so far as to admit that she wished

she could just stay at home and shop all day. At the time he'd thought it was a silly joke, but now he wasn't so sure. Maybe it helped explain her sudden change of heart.

Phil had always done nice things for Denise and given her plenty of shoes, bags, and jewelry, but as an educated man, he also knew that there had to be a limit. He knew he couldn't spend his retirement or his future kids' college tuition on the latest fashions.

"Maybe she just wanted more than I could give her," Phil said. "She had mentioned it once or twice, but I didn't take her seriously."

"What did you say when she did?"

"I told her that she better go get herself a ball player, but I didn't really mean for her to do it," Phil said as he laughed weakly.

"You still have feelings for her, don't you?"

"Of course I do. We were together for the last three years, and I knew her for a year or two before that." Phil braced himself. He knew that it was around this time that Marc would say something ridiculous or asinine.

"You still got the ring?"

"Yea, I haven't taken it back to the store yet," Phil said, but it was time and he knew it.

Shayla came back into the living room and brought each of the guys a beer.

Apprehensively, Phil asked, "So, about these friends of yours?"

"Let me at least get you guys something to eat first. Then we can get to that." Shayla stood. "I hope you like Mexican, Phil. I made my specialty, seven layer taco salad."

Marc perked up proudly and added, "And, man, the chips are homemade." He nodded as if he dared Phil not to believe him.

"Well, okay, Miss Shayla," Phil said. "I'll try some."

"Good," Shayla said then looked back at Marc. "And I know you want some." Her words were seductive as she winked and then went back to the kitchen.

Marc watched her walk away with a proud look on his face.

Shayla came right back into the dining room with the entrée and the side dishes.

"I like her for you, man," Phil said sincerely.

Phil's words caught both Marc and Shayla's attention. It was a nice compliment, but it created a little awkwardness in the room. Sensing it, Phil changed the subject.

"Now, about these friends of yours?"

"Yeah, babe, I was telling Phil how cool you and your girlfriends were. I suggested he maybe, you know, go out on a date with one."

Shayla relaxed a little. "Oh, okay. Well, I do have a few single girlfriends and they are all cute. What kind of women do you like?" she asked Phil.

"Set him up with one like you," Marc answered for Phil then clarified his statement. "Wait, that didn't come out right. I told him that most of your friends are just like you, so if he hung with us and got a feel of what you're like, he'd know it was safe to date one of your friends."

Shayla gave Marc the side eye. "Umm, I don't know if I like how that came out, but I think I understand." She fidgeted in her seat a little. "Makes me feel like I'm being graded, scrutinized, or something."

"Oh, no, it's nothing like that," Phil assured her. "It's just that, you know, birds of a feather flock together. Eagles don't fly with crows, so if your girlfriends are like you, I'd know your friends were good people too."

Shayla nodded, and they all dug in to the food she'd set before them.

After a while, Shayla looked at Phil and said, "Well . . ."

"The food is great," he answered.

She smiled at him. "That's not what I was asking."

Phil looked dumbfounded. Had he just failed some sort of test or something?

"Am I good people?" Shayla asked.

"The night is still young, but if I were a betting man, I'd go ahead and say that you were," he said.

"I've got it!" Marc said enthusiastically. "We'll have a cookout and pool party here next weekend."

"And I'll invite a few of my attractive and single friends," Shayla chimed in.

Phil was visibly skeptical, but he agreed. "All right, I guess. I don't have anything better to do."

"Bet, and I'll invite the strippers," Marc said with a sinister grin.

Shayla knew that he was only kidding, but she popped him on the arm anyway, just for good measure.

"The only person you get to see strip is me," she said with a tender authority.

Marc's ears perked up. "When?"

"You tell me," Shayla said with a smile as she gave him the sexiest look she could muster. She and Marc had momentarily forgotten that Phil was still there. They were having a full-fledged non-verbal conversation right in front of him, and he was certain that he didn't want to know what was being said.

"Welp! Time to go, Phil!" Marc said as he snapped out of the trance that Shayla had him in. "It's about that time. Text me and let me know that you made it home."

Marc stood up so as to help Phil expedite his departure.

"Wait. I was going to grab some more food," Phil protested.

"Kitchen's closed. I got some business to handle."

"Well, at least let me get a to-go plate," Phil insisted.

Marc grabbed a paper plate off the counter, set it on the table, took the spoon, and slapped a big scoop of the taco salad on it. Then, with his bare hand, he snatched a few chicken wings up and set them on the plate.

"One to-go plate, hot and ready, sir," Marc said as he handed it to Phil.

"You just going to touch my chicken like that?"

"Yep. Gotta go. Godspeed, my friend. See you in the morning at work." Marc ushered Phil out of the house.

Phil couldn't even be mad about it. He would probably have done the same thing. Plus, he was happy that Marc appeared to be settling down, even if it was only a little bit.

# Chapter 14

"You have arrived at your destination," Phil's GPS told him.

He passed by the address he'd been looking for, which was Shayla's house, and not for the usual reason, which was the fact that he had a terrible sense of direction. Neither was he having second thoughts about meeting one of her friends. He drove by it simply because there was nowhere to park.

Shayla had a hard time deciding which one of her single friends would be a good match for Phil. In her eyes, all of her friends were wifey material. To make it easier and more of Phil's decision rather than her own, she agreed with Marc's idea to just have a cookout at her house and invite all of her single female friends. That way Phil would have the opportunity to interact with them. If there was any type of connection, it would happen naturally. No setup.

Phil parked his car down the street and grabbed the bags of chips and six pack of beer he'd brought. As Phil approached Shayla's house, he could hear music, talking, and laughter coming from the backyard. He could also see a tent over the privacy fence. Since everyone looked to be out back having a good time, Phil walked to one side of the house rather than knocking on the front door. He pushed the gate open and entered the backyard.

All of the patio furniture was filled with guests chatting and laughing. There was more seating at two long picnic tables under the tent. Phil followed both his eyes and nose over to the grill that was smoking and the delicious aroma emanating from it. That's where he saw Marc, wearing a white grilling apron, with a spatula in hand, flipping burgers.

"That's how you feel, apron and all?" Phil asked as he approached Marc.

"My man. What's up?"

Since Marc was busy and Phil's hands were full, they gave each other a shoulder bump.

Phil gave Marc the once over and chuckled.

Marc laughed too. "We're doing this all for you." Marc spread his arms out and looked around.

Phil looked around as well. There were both men and women in attendance, but it was mainly women. Only a few of the women seemed to be there with a date, but Phil was grateful there were a few other men there. At least the purpose of the barbecue wouldn't be totally obvious. Phil didn't want to show up to a yard full of women waiting to be picked. The last thing he wanted was to participate in a ghetto episode of *The Bachelor*.

"There's some nice-looking women running around here, huh?" Marc smiled and nodded as he looked around.

Phil agreed. "I must say that Shayla has some nice-looking friends."

"You know, my girl has good taste in friends—and men, if I do say so myself. Of course, you already know most pretty chicks have fine friends." Marc had a smug look of conceit on his face.

"Oh, so she's your girl?" Phil teased. "Because I think that has slipped out of your mouth on more than one occasion. I'm starting to believe that it's no accident. Mr. Player-for-life is slowing down a little bit."

Marc's eyes bucked and he got nervous. "What? What are you talking about? Shayla and I are just having a good time, nothing serious."

"Phil, it's good to see you," Shayla said as she approached the two men carrying a pan of raw, seasoned chicken.

"It's good to see you too, Shayla." Phil looked around. "This is nice. Thank you so much for the invite."

"Not a problem." She looked to Marc. "You ready for the chicken, babe?"

Marc looked at the burgers on the grill. "Give me a couple minutes to get a few more of these burgers off."

"Okay," Shayla said. "I'll just take these back inside. Let me know when you're ready for them." Shayla kissed Marc on the cheek. "Thank you." She gave him googly eyes and then walked toward the house.

Phil stared at Marc, who was staring at Shayla as she walked away.

"Babe?" Phil said. "Did she just call you babe?" Phil was in complete disbelief. "And did you respond? Jesus, take the wheel!"

Marc turned and looked at Phil. "Naw, you're hearing things." He went back to flipping the burgers.

"Just like I'm hearing you refer to her as your girl. Naw, my brother, my hearing is just fine," Phil insisted. "I heard that with my good ear."

The two friends shared a laugh before a woman walked up to them.

"You must be Phil," she said.

Phil stopped laughing to give the beautiful woman standing in front of him his full attention. "Yes, I am," Phil said, taking in every detail. She was rocking a medium-sized curly fro. It framed her face nicely. Eyes, smile, teeth on point, she favored Kerry Washington.

"I'm Lisa," she said. "Shayla wanted me to let you know that you can put those beers in the cooler." She looked over toward the tent. "And you can just set the chips on one of the tables under the tent, where all the other food is at."

Phil looked down at the items he was still carrying. "Yes, ma'am."

"Then I'll lead the way," Lisa said. "Follow me."

Lisa turned to walk away. Even though her Capri cargo pants weren't tight, Phil could tell that she was active in somebody's gym a few days a week. She was carrying a bell-pepper back there, and Phil was an unapologetic ass man. He thought there was nothing sexier than a fine-looking woman with a nice ass.

"Go on, man," Marc whispered while nudging Phil.

"I'm going," Phil whispered back as he took his first step to follow Lisa.

"You can just place the chips right here." Lisa pointed to one of the tables under the tent, where several people were congregating and eating.

"Everything looks good," Phil said, eyeballing the food.

"It is," Lisa assured him with a small smirk. She knew he had peeked at her shape, and she had put a little extra on her walk, being that he was behind her. "I'll make you a plate after we put the beer up."

Phil was a little taken aback. "Oh, sure. That will be nice."

Lisa could hear the surprise in Phil's voice. "What? Never had a woman offer to fix you a plate before?" she guessed correctly. Denise never made his plates for him. She curled the hell out of his toes on occasion, but never really made his plates for him, even when she cooked.

Lisa walked off, heading for the cooler on the patio.

"Well, no—I mean yes. My mother," Phil said.

Lisa chuckled. "Well, I'm a Southern girl, originally from Alabama. Where I come from, the women fix the men's plates."

"A woman with Southern hospitality. I like that," Phil said as they arrived at the cooler.

Lisa lifted the lid for him and Phil placed the bottles into the ice.

"Thank you," Phil said.

"Anytime," Lisa replied.

There was a moment of awkward silence.

"Soooo." Lisa clasped her hands together. "How about that plate?"

"Oh, yes," Phil said, rubbing his belly. "I'm starved."

Phil followed Lisa over to the food, where she piled a plate high with all the things he said were his favorites. Phil took the plate and sat down at an empty spot at one of the tables under the tent. He took a bite of baked beans and then looked up to see that Lisa was just standing there.

"Aren't you going to eat?"

"Oh, no, I just had a plate. I'm going to let my food digest before I have a little more." She smiled.

"Oh, okay." Phil took a bite of his burger. He chewed, realizing that Lisa was still standing there smiling. "Uh, you can sit down and join me if you'd like."

"Oh, good. Thank you," Lisa said as she sat across from Phil. "I was just waiting on you to let me know it was okay to join you. I didn't want to sit down without you giving me permission."

Phil noted her use of the word "permission." It struck him as a little odd, since he'd never met a black woman who needed anybody's permission to do what she wanted. Still, he didn't want to pry. This was supposed to be a pleasant barbecue, not a therapy session for Shayla's friend.

After a few seconds, she asked, "Oh, do you need something drink?" She jumped up. "I can't believe I forgot to give you something to drink. I'm such a bad girlfriend."

Both Phil and Lisa nearly stopped breathing at Lisa's words. Realizing what she'd said, Lisa quickly tried to correct herself. "I mean a bad host." She swallowed hard. "Southern woman. Not a girlfriend." She let out a nervous laugh. "I mean, maybe someday I could end up being that, but definitely not right now. That would be stupid, right? I mean, I have a friend at work who met a guy one day, and three months later they were married. That was seventeen years ago, and they're still married. So, it could definitely happen. I know another . . ."

Lisa's words started to go in one of Phil's ears and out the other. She was in full ramble mode at this point. She had talked herself into a mild frenzy, and when she finally noticed that he had tuned her out, she got embarrassed and excused herself to the restroom.

Phil looked around and spotted Marc and Shayla over at the grill, putting the chicken on. He walked over to them.

"I see you were over there talking to Lisa," Shayla said, raising her eyebrows up and down. "She's nice, isn't she?"

"Oh, yes, definitely a nice girl," Phil agreed. "And boy, oh boy, can she talk."

Shayla chuckled. "Yes. She teaches kindergarten at the school I work at. Believe it or not, it only takes about two weeks for the kids to catch on and be able to follow and keep up with her. She definitely gives a new definition to fast learning."

"I bet," Phil said. "So you work at a school? I thought you were a nurse."

"I am," Shayla said. "I'm the school nurse."

Marc jumped in. "And she's the principal." Marc stood there wearing a proud grin.

"Oh, so you just running things," Phil said. "All the teachers and all the kids. I'm guessing that it can be stressful to say the least."

Shayla chuckled. "No, not really. I must say that I have a really nice group of kids and some excellent teachers." She looked over at Lisa, who was now talking somebody else's ear off. "And Lisa is one of them. You should really get to know her."

"I wouldn't mind getting to know her," Phil said. "It's her getting to know me that I'm afraid would never happen. I wouldn't be able to get a word in edgewise about myself. She either gets really talkative when she's nervous, or she loves the sound of her own voice. Either way, I believe that we would be better off just friends."

Shayla and Phil laughed together.

"Well, don't give up on her too quickly," Marc chimed in. "There might be some other amazing things she can do with that mouth."

"Marc!" Shayla said, elbowing him.

"I'm just saying." Marc chuckled.

Shayla shook her head. "He's you're friend," she said to Phil.

"Oh, no, don't put him on me," Phil said. "I am not responsible for his antics."

"Later for both of you," Marc said, turning his attention back to the grill.

"Well, I'm going to go finish this food." Phil held up his plate. "Walk around and mingle. I'll catch up with you two later."

Phil headed over to the patio area. He wasn't about to get hemmed up by Lisa again, so he kept an eye out for her. He did not have to spend any more time with her to know that they weren't a match.

Phil wasn't alone for long, as a nice-looking girl came over and sat down next to him. She introduced herself as Samantha, one of Shayla's friends. Phil looked over to where Shayla was standing, and she gave him a thumbs up and a wink. Phil knew Samantha was one of the girls Shayla was trying to set him up with.

"So, Samantha, don't tell me a nice-looking girl like you is single," Phil said.

She blushed. "Yep, I am."

Phil ate one of his potato chips. "Tell me, Samantha. Why are you single?" Phil didn't want to judge, but he was afraid that a woman this beautiful who was still single might have something crazy to say about it. In fact, her answer was pretty straightforward.

"Not all men love children."

Phil relaxed a little. That wasn't an issue for him. "I think kids are cool. I want to have a couple when I get married."

Samantha's eyes cast downward. "A couple is a little different than nine."

"Oh, you have a nine-year-old?" He took a bite of his burger.

"I have *nine* children," she said with emphasis.

Phil froze for a second, imagining the pure and utter chaos that it must be dealing with nine children, not to mention their fathers. He looked at Samantha again. That couldn't be right. She had to be a size six. No stretchmarks from what he could see under her midriff shirt. No way did nine people come out of her.

"That's right. I said I have nine children."

Phil paused. Apparently he'd done the math right. "Damn. So it doesn't even hurt anymore when you have a kid, does it? They just come swinging on out of there." He immediately regretted the comment. Marc and his sometimes crass ways were rubbing off on Phil.

Samantha giggled uncomfortably.

Sensing that his joke might have been more offensive to her than funny, Phil got serious. "I hope you don't mind me asking, but are they all by the same guy?"

Samantha squirmed a little, still showing signs of discomfort. "Not quite."

Phil swallowed a bite of his burger. Hard. "How many is not quite?"

Samantha held up her hand, fingers spread wide.

"Five?" Phil whispered loudly, nearly choking on the food he was chewing.

That was it as far as Phil was concerned. He knew that even if he could somehow find a way to care for this woman and her community center of kids, there was no way he would knowingly set himself up for a constant migraine in dealing with the five different fathers of these children.

Phil had to think quick. There had to be a way out of this. He looked off to the tent area. "Here I come." He stood up with his plate in hand. "I'll be right there." He took a step toward the tent, pretending to hear someone calling his name.

"Where are you going?" Samantha asked, confused. "I didn't hear anybody." She looked to see who might have been calling Phil away from her.

"Well, I did," Phil was quick to say as he exited stage left. He made his way back over to the tent area, passing Shayla along the way.

"So, how's it going?"

"It's not. She has a basketball team at home. If she plays, they've got five on five. No. Hell no."

Shayla chuckled. "It's not that bad."

"A woman with kids is not a deal breaker for me, but a woman with that many is."

Shayla loved her friend Samantha dearly. Phil could tell from the way she kept trying to sell him on her good qualities that Shayla really, truly just wanted to see Samantha happy.

Phil looked Shayla dead in the eye. "Shayla, she has given birth to nine children. After nine kids, I could probably toss my gym bag in there and she wouldn't even know it. It would be like throwing a hotdog down a hallway. No." He folded his arms defiantly.

"Okay, okay, I hear you," Shayla said. "Well, my friend Marcy is over there." She pointed to a clique of people engaging in laughter and conversation. "The one with the coral-colored shirt on," Shayla said. "She is cute, single, spiritual, and has only one kid."

Phil checked her out. "Now we're talking."

"Come on. I'll introduce you," Shayla said.

She walked Phil over to Marcy and made the introduction. Several minutes later, the two of them were alone. Phil and Marcy were leaning against the privacy fence, talking and laughing. Phil gave her the once over. Marcy was a little thicker than the other women he had met that night, but she owned her curves. She was confident, had a killer smile, and was still fine.

"It is so crazy that I'm meeting you tonight," Marcy said.

"Why is that?" Phil asked.

"God told me I was gonna meet my husband today."

Phil's eyes widened. He looked up at the heavens then looked back at Marcy. "So God just came right out and said that to you?"

Marcy nodded. "Yes. This morning while I was making breakfast. I heard God loud and clear. I was making my Nutribullet shake, like I do every morning, except as soon as I turned the blender on, I could hear his voice, plain as day."

"Are you sure it wasn't a small electric shock from the appliance that might have made you think you heard a voice?" Phil asked without a hint of humor in his voice.

Marcy laughed the thought off. "I wasn't electrocuted. I heard what I said I did."

Phil exhaled. Déjà vu time. "Here I come," he said as he started to walk away.

Marcy looked but didn't see anyone calling Phil. That got her excited. "Oh my goodness. He talks to you too?"

Phil just kept on walking as he said to himself, "Yep, and He just told me to leave your crazy ass alone."

Although Phil's food had gotten cold while he was trying to entertain all these women, he decided he was going to cop a spot alone, finish his meal, and call it a night.

That would have been too much like right. While he finished up his food, Shayla introduced him to a couple more of her friends. Both Phil and Shayla decided to take it easy on them and not make it so much of a hookup. Afterward, Phil still was 0 for 8. He was losing interest fast, and the comfort of his living-room recliner sounded great to him at that point.

Marc had finished at the grill, and came over to sit next to Phil.

Phil let out a deep breath. "Look, I appreciate what you and Shayla tried to do, but I don't think this was a good idea. Tell Shayla that's it. No more."

"Okay, but before you throw the towel in, you gotta meet Isabel."

Phil opened his mouth to decline, but Marc cut him off.

"Before you say no, she's not even one of Shayla's friends. She's a friend of a friend of a friend. I just met her tonight, and she is nice-looking and real cool. So what do you say? She could be the one you let get away."

"Or the one I'll need to run away from . . . again," Phil said.

"Come on, man," Marc pleaded, determined to find someone to take Phil's mind off of Denise.

Phil sighed. "Okay, but this is it. I'm done after this."

"Cool, come on. Turn around, because she's right behind you," Marc said as he directed Phil over to Isabel. "Isabel, I'd like you to meet Phil, a good friend of mine."

"Nice to meet you, Isabel," Phil greeted. He shook her hand, and she just stared at him, saying nothing for a moment.

Marc stood there watching them. He'd made the introduction. The rest was up to them.

Isabel was quiet as she stood there sizing Phil up, analyzing him from top to bottom. She slowly started walking around him like a lion circling its prey.

Finally, Isabel spoke to Phil. "Look at you. Good taste in clothes, shoes, and accessories. No excessive jewelry, but your Audemars wristwatch is a definite statement piece." She was on her second lap around him by now. "You're tall, got nice skin, good bone structure, and baby daddy hair."

Phil looked to Marc with questioning eyes. Marc shrugged his ignorance. Phil turned back to Isabel. "What is baby daddy hair?"

She continued staring at Phil, giving him a deep once over. "You're a breeder. We would make the prettiest kids. What are you doing later?"

Phil and Marc shared a knowing look. "Here I come," the two men said in unison as they rushed off. Once they were several feet away from Isabel, they burst out laughing.

"You so wrong for that," Phil said to Marc. "So wrong."

Marc feigned innocence. "What, Doctor Breeder?" He laughed.

"It ain't funny," Phil said.

"You're right." Marc stopped laughing. "It was funny as hell."

Phil and Marc busted out laughing again.

Once the laughter came to an end, Phil patted Marc on the back. "On the real, though, I appreciate you and Shayla, but I think I'm about to head out."

"Leaving so soon? But I just got here," said a voice coming from behind Phil and Marc.

Both men turned around.

Phil was shocked to see a familiar face. "Julie?"

She stood there carrying a store bought cake. She was looking extra nice in her a short romper outfit. This was the first time Phil had seen so much skin on Julie . . . so much beautiful brown skin. He couldn't help but allow his eyes to gaze over her. "What are you doing here?"

"Marc invited me," Julie answered. "Is that a problem or something?" She looked back and forth from Marc and Phil.

"Oh, no," Phil was quick to say. "It's just that I didn't know you were coming." He looked to his best friend. "Marc didn't mention it."

"You can thank me later," Marc said.

"I can't stay long though. Anthony needs the Jeep to do something later tonight."

"Anthony . . ." Phil said with a protective amount of curiosity. "Is he the guy that's been dropping you off and picking you up in your truck lately?"

"Yes. He and I have been dating for the last few weeks, and it's not a big deal about him driving my vehicle. He's looking for a job."

Phil and Marc had a brief, non-verbal conversation, and without a sound, they both agreed that something wasn't right. They had been around each other for so many years that they could shoot a look to the other one and no words ever needed to be said.

Julie's phone started vibrating in her purse, so she stepped away from Phil and Marc to answer the call.

Phil motioned to Julie to get her attention. "Marc and I are going to grab a drink, you want one?" he said in a low voice.

Julie signaled for Phil to hold on a moment. Her gesture had a sense of urgency attached to it, so although he wanted to walk away, he stayed close and started paying more attention to her.

"Nobody. That was just Phil, from the office. I work with him, or for him, or both. He was just asking if I wanted something to drink." Julie softened her voice a little so she could get some semblance of privacy. "I've worked with him for years now. You don't have anything to worry about."

Phil tapped Marc on the arm to get his attention, interrupting his gawking session. He was staring at a group of women like he had never seen a nice ass or two before.

"What do you think that's about?" Phil asked, shifting his eyes in Julie's direction.

From her body language and the soft tension in her voice, both men could sense there was definitely something wrong with her situation.

"Then you should have come with me if you're really that worried about it. I invited you, but no! You didn't want to come," Julie snapped back at whoever was on the other end of the call.

Phil could see from the look on Julie's face that whatever was just said on the phone had her shook. She was speaking very gingerly, in almost a full whisper.

"I'm not getting smart with you. I just—Yes, I remember what you said, and I'm sorry. I just got here, though. Okay, I'm on the way," Julie said, completely dejected as she hung up her phone and slid it back in her handbag.

Phil and Marc were doing a terrible job of pretending not to have heard the conversation when Julie walked back over to them.

"I have to go, guys. I'm sorry," Julie said.

"Anything we can do to help?" Phil asked.

"No, but thank you," Julie said as she attempted to smile at Phil.

Phil and Marc watched her leave, not out of appreciation for her shape or her beauty, but genuine concern for her happiness and her well-being.

"Something's going on with her," Phil said.

"I know," Marc replied.

"We'll check on her tomorrow. I'm going to get out of here too. I'll see you at work, brother," Phil said as he started to leave.

He found Shayla on the way out and thanked her again for helping set all of this up for him. She had a good heart. Phil knew that Marc had a good woman. He was happy for him, and he hoped and prayed for Marc's sake that he wouldn't mess it up. Phil was afraid that Shayla was the only thing still holding Marc together. Maybe Marc had really turned over a new leaf. Or maybe some things never change.

# Chapter 15

"Doctor Gooden! Doctor Gooden!"

Phil had just gotten out of his car and was hitting the key fob to lock the door when he heard his name being called out. He looked to see one of his patients doing a light jog toward him.

"Mr. Hartfield," Phil said. "I didn't realize I had an appointment with you today."

"You don't," Mr. Hartfield said, catching his breath. "I was on my way to work and was hoping I could catch you. I couldn't wait until my next appointment to tell you this."

Phil didn't know whether to be concerned, afraid, or to just listen. He decided to go with option C, because Mr. Hartfield looked happier and more excited than Phil had ever seen him. His energy was contagious, so much so that a smile spread across Phil's face just looking at his patient.

"What's going on? Looks like you just hit the lottery," Phil said.

"Nope." Mr. Hartfield shook his head. "Even better." All of a sudden he got serious and looked around as if someone might be watching them. He leaned in and whispered something in Phil's ear. When he pulled back, that huge Kool-Aid grin was once again covering his face.

A huge and proud smile spread across Phil's face. "So it worked? Because the last time we talked, her doing that for you was out of the question."

"It was," Mr. Hartfield confirmed. "But not anymore. Thanks to me doing a lot of things I didn't want to do, like cleaning up, pushing a vacuum, and wearing that cologne she bought me, she's doing a lot of things that she didn't do. And I did what you suggested. After dinner, I gave her the remote, walked her over to the couch, sat her down, and I cleaned the dishes. She damn near lost her mind. My wife barely even let me finish before she attacked me."

Phil nodded. "Well, I'm happy for you, man. You deserve it. Just remember, the hard part, pardon the pun, is to be consistent with it—with your effort, your energy. You are going to have to continue challenging yourself to keep finding new and creative ways to show her that she is the love of your life and that she is still every bit as beautiful and sexy as she was when you fell in love with her. You do that, and chores or not, you will get what you need from your mate."

Phil was genuinely happy to hear that his patient was making progress in his marriage. No, it wasn't usual for one of his patients to run up on him without an appointment to report that his wife was now giving him head again, but hell, a success story was a success story.

"You're happy? I'm ecstatic!" Mr. Hartfield confirmed.

"I bet you are," Phil said. "I'm truly glad to hear that my advice from our session is working out for you."

"Me too. I can't wait until my next one. I've been trimming the bushes, washing the car. Hell, if I keep it up, she just might let me go through the back door!" he exclaimed.

Phil put his hands up and gave Mr. Hartfield a look. "Whoa, whoa. Too much information, man. TMI."

"Oh, my bad."

Phil chuckled. "Well, make sure you give Julie a call so we can get you scheduled."

"I already did!"

Phil was exceptionally glad to hear that Mr. Hartfield didn't plan on stopping his sessions just because things seemed to be going in his favor. That was one of the major issues Phil had, and he had discussed it with other therapists. Sometimes when things seemed to be going well or the patients thought they were "fixed," they would stop coming to sessions, not realizing that the same way they had to keep a car in good condition, they should do the same with their mind, spirit, and soul. It was important to have an outlet to vent and discuss the things that they couldn't talk about with anyone else. Sometimes, even when life seemed bearable, it still didn't hurt to seek out counseling. Phil liked to call it preventative maintenance.

"Then I guess I'll be seeing you soon," Phil said.

"You sure will." He looked Phil in the eyes while he vigorously shook his hand. "Thank you again, Dr. Gooden. I truly do mean that from the bottom of my heart."

Phil smiled, nodded, and then watched Mr. Hartfield practically skip off to his car. Sure, the monetary benefits of this job were plentiful, but moments like that were the real payoff. Phil knew that if he hadn't been able to help Mr. Hartfield, there was a very good chance he and his wife were headed for divorce, due to both of them being unhappy, or Mr. Hartfield's eventual infidelity. Phil knew that when a man wasn't getting what he used to get or what he needed at home from his wife, fiancée, or girlfriend, he would start to look outside the home.

It was like the 80/20 rule that Phil had heard Bishop T.D. Jakes speak about. He said that the closest you will ever get to your ideal mate is eighty percent. The only one hundred percent person was Jesus. But sometimes, folks get comfortable, lazy, and complacent and begin to take that eighty percent for granted. At some point, they may see in another person the characteristics of the twenty percent that's missing in their relationship. From the right angle, when the sun hits it just right from a distance, that twenty percent shines brightly and looks like that one hundred percent they have been looking for. They leave their soul mate, their eighty percent, and chase down that twenty percent, only to find out that it's really just a fraction of what they already had at home.

Phil was recharged, having been able to help Mr. Hartfield get excited about his wife again and vice versa. Not every man out there was like Mr. Egan, just looking to score. Mr. Hartfield was proof of that. He just wanted his wife back, and if that meant that he had to step up his game, then he was willing to do it.

Mr. Hartfield's energy had definitely transferred over to Phil as he headed toward the office building. Halfway to the office door, he heard the sound of loud music. It only seemed to get louder, until it was right upon Phil. As Phil opened the lobby door, a shiny, black Jeep Cherokee with tinted windows came to a stop in the parking lot behind him. He turned around to see Julie getting out of the passenger's side. The driver attempted to lean over and kiss her, but she was clearly having none of it.

As Julie walked around the front of the truck, adjusting her shades, the passenger window rolled down. That's when Phil was able to see Julie's chauffer. At first Phil thought that he was rolling down the window to give Julie one last good-bye, but instead he glared at Phil.

He paused the music. "All right then, baby," Anthony said to Julie. "I'll see you tonight." He turned his attention back to Phil. Once again, Anthony was making his presence known in Julie's life, just in case one of her coworkers, namely her boss, got any ideas about trying to get with Julie.

It was an insecure move and Phil knew it, but he didn't understand why. He had made no moves on Julie whatsoever, so in his mind, it was all unnecessary.

Julie didn't respond or even look back. Something was definitely wrong on the home front, but Phil thought it would be in bad taste to pry. He would wait until Julie wanted to talk about it, if she ever did.

Instead of walking right in, Phil held the door for Julie. He was sure that Anthony wouldn't like that he did it, but he was a gentleman first and foremost.

"Thank you," Julie said as she moseyed on by him into the lobby.

Phil bit his tongue so as not to say anything about the obvious tension he had just witnessed. He was about to head inside, but then he saw Marc pulling up. He checked his watch.

"What?" Phil said to himself in a surprised tone. It was ten 'til nine. It was Marc's M.O. to arrive at work only five to ten minutes prior to his first appointment, and he never made appointments before ten.

"My eyes must be deceiving me," Phil said once Marc had gotten out of his car and was making his way toward the door. "You do know it's not time to set the clocks ahead. It really is only going on nine o'clock."

"You know what? I'ma let your little snide remark slide," Marc said, wearing a freshly pressed suit and carrying his briefcase. "I plan on having a great day, and I'm not going to let anyone mess it up. Not even you."

Phil simply stood back and smiled while Marc marched up the walkway looking open-casket sharp. He couldn't help but laugh. If he had to be honest, though, confidence looked good on Marc. Was it possible he really was turning over a new leaf? Why now?

"You know, you are the second person today to come here looking all McHappy," Phil said. "And with the last person who showed up like this, it had to do with a woman. Can I assume the same goes for my best friend?" Phil shot Marc a knowing look.

"Why can't it just be because life is good?" Marc asked.

"I can't argue with that, I guess. Brotha, if you breathing, you're doing good. There are some folks that didn't even wake up this morning."

"Then they should have set their alarm like me," Marc bragged. "But if you must know, I have to take a long lunch today, so I figured I'd come in a little early to make up the time."

"Make up the time how? By sitting at your desk updating your social media? You never make appointments this early, and I know you don't have a client coming this early."

Marc held his arms out wide. "Don't I look like a changed man to you? I told you I'm going to start doing better, and I am. And it ain't got nothing to do with a woman." Marc walked into the lobby.

"Well, Mr. New Man, try scheduling your appointments earlier. You'd be surprised how many more patients you can take in a week, which equals more money."

"I'll take your suggestion under advisement." Marc turned to Phil and gave him a nod.

"Yeah, and make sure you do, because you know what they say," Phil said. "The early bird catches the worm."

"Oh, yeah," Marc answered, "but the second mouse gets the cheese. First one gets caught in the trap. Hashtag, *message!*" Marc said with a laugh.

"Man, get in there and let's go to work," Phil said playfully and pointed to Marc's office door.

This had been a nice start to Phil's day. He'd bumped into more people and had more excitement in the parking lot than he did sometimes in the office. Little did he know, things were just getting started.


"Julie, can you step in my office for a minute?" Phil asked her over the intercom. He decided he'd chat with Julie for a minute before he went to lunch.

A few seconds later, Julie entered his office. "What's up, boss?"

Phil looked up from his calendar. "Boss? Since when am I 'boss'? And why do you still have your sunglasses on?" He looked up at the lights. "Should I switch out the hundred-watt bulbs to sixty?" He laughed, but her behavior did seem a bit odd to him. She had been wearing sunglasses when she came in this morning, but he certainly hadn't expected her to be wearing them inside all day.

Julie shrugged and chuckled, trying to brush off his question. "I had a late night. Don't want the clients thinking I've been hanging out with Marc."

"Okay, but why so formal with the whole 'boss' thing?" Phil asked.

"I don't know. I was just being funny, I guess."

"Being funny, huh?"

Julie stood there smiling awkwardly. Then finally she said, "Soooo, did you need something?"

In Phil's opinion, Julie seemed a little nervous.

"Are you okay?" Phil asked.

"I'm good. Just think I've been overdoing it with the late hours at work, and I'm going to start cutting that back a bit. I need a little more me time."

"Are you sure?" Phil asked, sensing that she was concealing something. "You know you can talk to me about anything."

"I'm fine, Phil. Thanks for asking. I have a bunch of work to take care of if I'm going to actually make it out of here on time today, so I'd better get to it."

"Okay. Let me know if you need anything."

Phil watched Julie leave the room, knowing that she was just as stubborn as he was and that she had no intention of telling him what was wrong. He couldn't tell why she was holding back, but he was determined to get to the bottom of it soon enough.

The rest of the work day went well. Marc was unusually quiet and professional with his clients. Julie was heavily preoccupied with her work and with the wall that Phil caught her staring at a couple of times. Something in his spirit told him to push the envelope. Besides, Julie still had those sunglasses on. She had worn them all day. Phil had counseled many battered and abused women and Julie's behavior was throwing up all kinds of red flags for him now.

Phil had focused on his patients and been able to keep all these thoughts at bay during the day, but now that his last appointment of the day had left, it was time to take the gloves off. Phil eased out to Julie's desk and stopped directly in front of her. She was gathering her things so she could leave for the day, so it startled her when she finally did notice that he was there.

"Julie, I need you to take those glasses off for a second, please."

Julie grabbed her purse and her jacket and kept looking around her desk. "Where are my keys?" she mumbled to herself. Julie was starting to get worked up about not being able to find them.

"Anthony dropped you off today, remember? He probably has them."

"You know what? You're right."

"Good. Now can you please take the sunglasses off?"

"I can't. Anthony will be here any minute to pick me up, and I don't want to be late."

Julie tried to head for the door, but Phil cut her off and stopped in front of her. She stopped dead in her tracks.

"Julie, the glasses. Now."

Julie's shoulders slumped as the fight left her. She slowly raised her left hand and removed her shades, revealing a black eye and a bruised cheek. The sight of this infuriated Phil, but he wanted to be sure not to take it out on Julie.

"Anthony did that to you?"

Julie looked down and said nothing.

"Is this the first time he put his hands on you?"

Again, Julie didn't say a word, but the look of hurt and shame on her face, and the single tear that slowly dropped from that injured eye, said it all. Phil grabbed a tissue from the box on her desk and handed it to her.

Phil looked at his watch. It was five p.m. on the dot.

"He's downstairs waiting on you right now?"

Julie nodded her head.

"You stay up here and wait until I get back. You hear me?"

"Yes," Julie whispered.

"I'm going with you!" Marc declared. He had walked into the lobby not long after Phil and had witnessed the whole conversation. He was just as pissed as Phil.

The two men headed out of the room, walking with a quiet rage, only stopping to take off their suit jackets.

Phil and Marc made it to the parking lot in no time, only to find Anthony leaning against Julie's Jeep. His outfit was typical: saggy blue jeans, a wife-beater, and some knock-off Timberlands. He was brown-skinned, bald-headed, about six feet two, 225 pounds. He had a toothpick in his mouth and he was giving off pure attitude.

Both Phil and Marc had only seen glances of him when he was dropping off or picking up Julie, but they were pretty sure that this was the son of a bitch that had hit Julie, most likely more than once. Phil and Marc walked over to Anthony, stopping three feet in front of him, looking him in the eye.

"You're Anthony, right?"

"Yeah," Anthony replied nonchalantly.

"We work with Julie," said Marc, chiming in.

"Oh, so y'all secretaries too," Anthony said with a sneer.

"That's funny," Phil replied with everything except humor in his eyes.

Phil wasn't in the mood for verbal jousting, especially with a cowardly abuser like him.

"What happened to Julie's face?"

"You know, couples have problems sometimes."

"So you hit her!" Mark said sternly as he inched closer to the man they both wanted to hurt badly. Phil put his arm out, keeping him at bay. Phil had always been the cool, calm, collected one of the two. Things needed to remain that way, at least for the moment.

Anthony spit out his toothpick and looked back and forth between them. "It ain't really none of your concern."

Phil stepped a little closer to Anthony. "That make you feel good, hitting on a woman? Make you feel like a man?"

Anthony stood up straight and puffed out his chest. He twisted up the corners of his mouth and nodded his head with a shoulder shrug. "So I hit her. Isn't it obvious that we kissed and made up? I don't even know why I'm out here talking to you two clowns. It's not really your concern now, is it? What y'all trying to do, out here making me look like the bad guy so y'all can get at Julie? I know how you suits work. Acting like some ol' jealous bitches. Y'all might as well be wearing skirts. Like I said, it's not your business."

"It is now," Phil said as he was rolling up the sleeves on his dress shirt. "Hit me!" Phil barked as he got face-to-face with Anthony.

"Naw, man, I don't have any problem with you."

"What, you scared that I'm going to hit back? Hit me!" Phil yelled.

Anthony got right up in Phil's face, breathing heavily.

"I said this ain't about you, but if you don't get out my face, it's gonna be." A look of rage covered Anthony's face. He balled his fist and veins began popping out of his head as he stood there breathing hard.

Phil looked Anthony in the eye and right through him. The time for words was over.

"Don't say I didn't give you a chance," Phil said calmly as he took half a step backward and motioned for Marc to back up and let him handle it.

Anthony cracked a crooked smile, but Phil punched him in it before it could turn into a full smirk. Anthony was a big boy, so just as Phil expected, he didn't drop from the first punch. Instead, he drew back and threw a wild haymaker that Phil could see coming from a mile away.

Phil slipped to his left, avoiding the punch. He fired off a heavy left-handed hook that rocked Anthony, but he still didn't go down. Phil followed up with a hook to the body and an uppercut to Anthony's chin, which finally knocked him down to his hands and knees.

Phil looked over at Marc, who was salivating at the chance for his shot at Anthony.

"You want to get some of this?" Phil said.

Even though Marc hated to kick a man when he was down, literally, he figured what the hell. Anthony wasn't a man. He was a woman beater. "Hell yeah, I thought you'd never ask."

Phil reached out his hand and tagged Marc in, like they did in professional wrestling.

"Tag," Marc said as he started to go to work on Anthony with heavy punches and kicks.

Suddenly, Marc just stopped hitting Anthony and paused, as if in thought. Perhaps he figured that Anthony had taken enough abuse. He began to walk around the front of the Jeep. All the while Phil looked on, not quite sure of what Marc was doing.

"You know something, Anthony?" Marc said while passing the passenger's side of the truck. "What goes around . . . Always comes—" Marc had passed the back of the Jeep and was picking up speed as he arrived back to Anthony. "Back around!" Marc yelled as he kicked the hell out of Anthony's midsection. Marc turned to Phil to make sure that he hadn't gone too far. Phil gave him an approving nod.

"Now that's how you whip somebody's ass," Phil said with a satisfied grin.

"This is Julie's truck, right?" Marc asked Phil.

"Yep."

Marc reached in Anthony's pocket and grabbed the keys and handed them to Phil.

"I'm taking the truck key and the apartment key," Phil said, removing them from the key ring as he was talking. "You're moving out today. Julie is going to leave all your belongings in a bag out front. Don't knock, don't ring the bell, and don't call. Just grab your stuff and go. I promise you, this is nothing compared to what we are going to do to you if you bother her again. You understand?"

"Yeah," Anthony whispered in defeat.

Phil tossed the half-empty key-ring on Anthony's chest then stood up. He and Marc walked toward the building, chirping the alarm on Julie's Jeep as they did. Phil hoped that was the last any of them would see of Anthony.

# Chapter 16

As soon as Phil sat down at his desk, his phone rang. He checked his caller ID before answering the phone.

"Pops. What's going on?" Phil greeted.

"Hey, son," Mr. Gooden said.

"How's it going?"

"That's what I'm calling to ask you. I haven't seen you in a minute."

"Yeah, I know." Phil hated to admit it. He was usually good about checking in on his parents pretty often, but he'd been so caught up with his own issues that he hadn't done so. Usually, no matter how hectic it got for him, he made time for a short weekly conversation. Phil had had clients with such horrible relationships with their parents that it had actually been years since they'd seen their parents. That had been a constant reminder to appreciate the good parents he had been blessed with. "I talked to Mom last week, though."

"What was your mother talking about?" his father asked.

"The two of you, actually. I asked her how things were between you guys."

"You didn't tell her what you and I talked about, did you?" He sounded a little paranoid.

"No, Pops. Keeping people's trust is what I do for a living. I don't betray the complete trust of strangers, so I sure wouldn't do it with my own flesh and blood," Phil said. "We did talk about her issues, though. I got her to tell me about the meds. She and I three-way called her doctor. We got her medicine situation taken care of. The doctor says for her to give her new medicine a trial period and then he'll go from there."

"That's actually what I was calling you about," Mr. Gooden said. "Your mother and I have been pretty good. We haven't had an argument in a month, and that's good for us." He let out a laugh.

"That's good to hear, Pops."

"Yeah, after talking to you, I became a little more understanding. Guess I was being selfish, you know. But that's how us Gooden men are. We want what we want. It's our way or the highway. Sometimes if you sacrifice and just give the other person what they want, it makes them happy, and in a roundabout way, it makes you happy. Happy wife, happy life. It's as easy as that."

Little did Mr. Gooden know that he'd just passed on some advice of his own to his son.

"You know what, Pops? You are absolutely right," Phil said. "Hey, what do you say I take you and Mom out to dinner? I'll check my calendar, get with Mom, and we'll make it happen."

"That would be nice. It's been a while since we've been out for a meal. You bringing Denise along?"

Phil didn't want to break the news about the breakup over the phone. "I'm not sure if she'll be able to make it, Pop, but I definitely will."

"Okay, sounds like a plan. I'll tell your mother the good news, and I'll talk to you later, son."

"Okay. I love you, Dad. Tell Ma that I love her too," Phil said with a smile.

"We love you too, son."

Phil hung up the phone with a smile on his face. It didn't last long, though, because he realized that he was going to have to tell his parents that the engagement was off. This wouldn't have been so difficult except that he knew his mom was excited about finally having some grandkids. He would have to figure out a way to tell them.

It had been a long day for Phil and eventful in every way. It was definitely one of those days where he wanted to get out of the office on time like everyone else, but he really needed to make some notes in the file of his last client of the day, while everything was still fresh in his mind. He wasn't looking forward to writing the notes, because even with the Advil he had taken, his hands still hurt.

Phil exhaled. He'd had patients who took months, sometimes years, to see the light and get help for their abusive situation or to leave the abuser altogether. Some never got help and never got away, and they were still living in fear and hell to this day. He had one patient whose husband discovered that she'd been secretly receiving therapy when the insurance company, through his job, sent him a statement. He followed his wife to an appointment and literally dragged her out of Phil's office. The police were called, but nothing ever came of it because Phil's patient wouldn't give a statement against her husband or be a witness against him. Phil said that he would testify based on what he'd witnessed with his own eyes, but the board thought it would be a slippery slope as far as doctor-patient privileges went. Phil had fought with the board, saying that he'd rather lose his license than for his client to lose her life.

"You can't help someone who doesn't want to be helped," was the board's consensus. "No matter what you do or don't do, this woman is going to lie down in bed next to her husband every night, while you're boxing up and clearing out your office."

Phil hated to admit it, but those words rang true. It still haunted Phil to this day, wondering whatever became of his former patient. Hopefully her decision hadn't cost her life. One thing he was sure of was that he was not going to relive that nightmare with Julie. No matter what.

# Chapter 17

The next day, Phil walked into the lobby and was glad to see Julie happily working at her desk. She looked much more like herself. Phil walked over to the edge of her desk.

"How are you doing this morning?" he asked. Last evening when he'd dropped her off at her place, she'd still been a little shaken up. Phil had offered to sit with her, but she declined, assuring him that she'd be okay. That didn't stop him from checking on her place several times during the night, making sure Anthony didn't get any bright ideas.

Julie looked up at Phil. "Actually, I'm all right," she said with sincerity.

"He didn't try to come back last night, did he?" Phil inquired as he took a closer look at her eye.

Julie shook her head. "Nope, he grabbed his bag of things that I set on the porch and left. I think you and Marc did a good job of making sure that he wouldn't be back." Julie then said sternly, "Not that I agree with violence." She softened her facial expression. "But thank you."

"You're welcome," Phil said. "And for the record, we're family around here. No need to thank us. Family is supposed to have each other's backs. So if another man puts his hands on you and you don't tell somebody, I'ma hit you upside the head my damn self. Okay?" He laughed.

"Okay," Julie said with a soft smile.

"Let me know if you need anything, Jewels."

Phil froze, realizing that he had just given Julie a nickname. Not only had he done that, but he had said it out loud. There was a brief and uncomfortable silence. The smirk on Julie's face gave away the fact that she had caught the term of endearment. Phil was thankful that she didn't say anything about it.

"Is Marc in yet?" Phil knew damn well Marc had never beat him into work a day in his life, but he needed something to change the subject.

"As a matter of fact, he is," Julie replied.

"What?" Phil said, shocked. "I didn't expect that."

"Then why'd you ask?" Julie teased.

Realizing she was on to his failed attempt at trying to change the subject, he made one more effort to do it. "I need to talk with him real quick before my first patient comes." Phil hurried off toward Marc's office.

"Got a lot of energy this morning, Doctor Gooden," Julie said, looking down at some papers on her desk. "Especially for someone who was up most of the night."

Phil stopped in his tracks. "Hey, how do you know what I—?"

He stopped talking when Julie looked at him with a knowing look in her eyes. "Thanks, Phil. I saw you drive by my place a few times last night to check on me. I slept a little better knowing you were watching out for me," she said with a smile then turned her attention back to her papers.

Phil smiled, nodded, and then went to Marc's office. He had been there at Julie's place three times the night before. She was more than just a coworker; she was a friend and damn near family to him. There was no way in hell he was going to let that poor excuse of a man hurt her anymore.

What Julie didn't know was that Phil was also a licensed gun owner and he could carry a concealed weapon almost anywhere and anytime. Had something jumped off last night, had Anthony limped his sorry ass back to try to hurt Julie again, Phil was locked and loaded. He was more than prepared to put a permanent end to the situation, but at this point, he was also glad that he hadn't had to go to that extreme.

Phil knocked on Marc's open door and walked into his office. Initially he hadn't really needed Marc for anything. In fact, he hadn't even expected that Marc would be into work this early, but since he was, he was going to give him his props for it.

"Hey, my man, what's up?" Phil asked cheerfully. The pride in his voice and approval of his best friend was short lived. "YouTube. You really sitting in here on YouTube this morning? "

"Shhh. This video is hilarious," Marc said, staring intently at the screen.

Phil just watched him, shaking his head, but he decided not to give him any grief about it. As long as he wasn't doing that when there were patients in session, it was okay.

Phil looked around Marc's office. It had the potential to be a really nice office, but Marc had just the bare essentials in there. There was his desk and chair, and two arm-chairs in front of his desk for the patients to sit in, a five-drawer file cabinet, and nothing else. There was a baseball glove hanging on a nail, next to a cat calendar, which was two years old and had actually been there when Phil bought the building.

"I'm definitely glad that you're dressing the part now," Phil said. "At some point very soon, though, we need to do something about this office. We need to get a coffee table and some nicer chairs in here, and maybe a sofa.

Remember, the more comfortable your patient is, the more likely they are to actually open up to you."

"I know. I'll get on it," Marc said with a knowing smile.

"Thank you. And can you pick up a painting or two for your walls? The cat calendar isn't the business."

"I like it."

Phil shot Marc a look.

"Okay, fine, I'll lose the damn calendar."

"Thank you. One more thing before I go. You got a number on that Mariah Quinton girl?"

Marc stopped messing with his smartphone and focused. "Why do I know that name?"

"She's the patient you fell asleep on last week. The one that burst out of the office crying. You were supposed to call and check on her. Did you?"

Marc's eyes floated down to his desk. "My bad, man. It totally slipped my mind, but the number should be in the file. I'll give her a call now."

"That's okay, I'll do it. Where are her case file and her session tapes?"

Marc apprehensively grabbed the requested items from his file cabinet and handed them to Phil. The look on his face was proof that he knew he had dropped the ball.

"Thank you," Phil said as he left Marc in the office alone with his thoughts. Phil figured that sometimes, silence was more effective than chewing someone out.

Phil got back to his office and sat down at his desk. He popped the audio tape of the last session in the tape player, rewound it a little, and then pressed play.

He flipped through the file while he listened to the tape. Mariah's dialogue grabbed his attention, so much so that he stopped flipping through her file and just listened as Mariah's words filled the room.

"I just feel like I'm here all alone." Her voice emanated from the recorder. "Like I don't matter. I can be in a room full of people and still be lonely. One would think it would make me sad, but it doesn't. It makes me angry. I feel like I could scream as loud as I can. And sometimes, I do just that. . . . But no one ever hears me. I bet if I was gone they'd hear me. I bet they'd wish they had listened then."

Her sincere words abruptly fell off, and she gasped.

"Wow! I'm paying you to listen to me, and you can't even stay awake," she said angrily. "Thanks a lot, Doc." Phil heard some rustling around on the tape, and then a loud door slam. It sounded so real and present that Phil jumped and turned his attention to the doorway. He was startled to see Julie standing there.

"Sorry. Didn't mean to eavesdrop," she said, standing in the doorway. "That was deep." Julie nodded to the recorder. She'd heard the tape. She looked to Phil. "Maybe we shouldn't have let her leave that day."

"You're telling me," Phil said, feeling regretful.

Phil hit the intercom button on the phone and asked Marc to step into his office. Marc walked in smiling, but once he saw the look on Phil's and Julie's faces, he quit grinning and stopped in his tracks.

"What's up?"

Phil exhaled, trying his best not to fly off the handle and speak disrespectfully to his friend.

"Did you even go back and listen to the part of the session that you slept through?" Phil asked, knowing the answer. There was no way Marc could have heard Mariah's words and not been alarmed and done something about it. At least Phil hoped that wasn't the case.

Marc confirmed with a shake of his head that he hadn't listened to the tape.

"So you haven't checked on her at all?" Phil asked for clarification.

"I'm sorry," was all Marc could say.

"She pretty much left you a suicide note, but because you were out all night the night before, you slept right through it. You're my boy, man, but this is some bullshit." He snatched the file from in front of Marc and headed for the door. "Julie, cancel my morning appointments." He stopped and pointed at Marc. "You better hope she's all right." He balled his fist. "I mean, you better hope to God this girl didn't do anything stupid."

Julie looked at Marc with disdain as she said to Phil, "Hold up. Let me cancel the appointments real quick, but I'm going with you."

Phil and Julie left Marc alone with his own silence. He was realizing the gravity of the situation.

"Fuck!" he yelled, throwing a pen across the room. He'd messed up big time for sure. He figured he might as well start packing up his office.


Julie read Mariah's address from her file to Phil, and he put it in the GPS. Forty minutes later, the two were at Mariah's front door. Both were nervous as all get out, not knowing what to expect.

Phil took a deep breath and then knocked on the door. A few moments passed, and there was no response. Phil stood there with a horrible feeling in the pit of his stomach.

"Try it again," Julie urged him.

He knocked again. Still there was no answer.

This time Julie rang the doorbell. "What if she's at work or something? Maybe there's a work number in her file."

"Yeah, you're right," Phil said, a glimmer of hope in his eyes. He turned to leave the porch so that he could go back to the car to retrieve the file. That's when they heard a clicking sound.

Both turned their attention to the door as it opened. They didn't exhale too quickly, as they first had to see who was on the other side of the door.

Through a small crack in the door, someone said, "Whatever it is, I already have it or I don't want it."

"Wait, please!" Phil yelled. "Mariah?" he said, not one hundred percent sure it was her since he could barely see her; but the voice sounded familiar.

The door opened wider. "Who are you?" Mariah asked Phil.

Mariah's appearance gave Phil pause. Her spirit was visibly broken, as a dark shadow seemed to be cast over her. Her eyes were red, with bags under them.

He pretended as though the way she looked had gone unnoticed by him. "It's me, Dr. Gooden," Phil said. He stepped to the side so that she could see Julie. "And this is Julie, my secretary. Do you remember her from the office? She works for Doctor Collins."

She went to close the door again.

"Please, Mariah, no," Phil pleaded. "I didn't come to try to get you to see Dr. Collins. I came to see about you myself," Phil told her.

"Yes, Mariah," Julie assured her. "We were worried about you."

Phil realized that it may be easier for her to relate to another woman, so he took half a step back, allowing Julie to take the lead. He was thankful that she had known what the look in his eyes meant.

"Is it okay if we come in for a minute?" Julie gave a sympathetic smile.

Mariah's eyes traveled up and down Julie's body before she opened the door all the way. "Sure. Come on in." She didn't sound too excited about letting them in, but Phil or Julie were relieved that she was allowing it nonetheless.

They stepped into Mariah's apartment and she closed the door behind them.

"You'll have to excuse the place." She looked around, seemingly disgusted herself by what she saw, as if it was her first time seeing it. More than likely, it was her first time mentally taking note of it. Depression could do that to a person.

Phil stayed focused on Mariah, while Julie couldn't help but look at the clothes and clutter strewn about the living room. Mariah's eyes drifted over to the coffee table, and she quickly swooped up something before Julie or Phil got a chance to see what it was. With the way that place looked, it could have been anything.

There weren't any dishes or old food packages lying around. Mariah had probably been too depressed to even eat. Julie wondered, though, how in the world one's living room filled up with clothes and shoes. Perhaps the bedroom, but the living room? Julie figured Mariah must have been just existing, forcing herself to go out, and then not even having the strength to make it to her bed, so the living room had become her living quarters.

"Mind if I ask why you're here?" Mariah walked over to the couch and began clearing it off. "This isn't how it usually works. The patient comes to the doctor; the doctor doesn't come to the patient. So why do I get the special treatment?"

"Maybe you're special." Phil nodded, not wanting to come on too strong, but wanting to start the emotional rebuilding process right away.

Mariah stared at him for a moment and then began to laugh. "Ha! Good one. Me special? Yeah, right."

Neither Phil nor Julie responded. They just stood there and allowed Mariah to get it out of her system.

Mariah stopped laughing. "I know the courts didn't send you. I'm done with them. Fulfilled my obligation to them at the last visit. You know, the one where I interrupted your partner's nap time."

Phil looked down at the floor, embarrassed by Marc's actions. "I can't apologize enough for my colleague," Phil said regretfully, looking at Mariah.

"You're right. You can't."

"But this isn't about him, Mariah," Phil said. "Whatever Dr. Collins did or didn't do doesn't matter anymore. But you matter, and what you have to say matters. I know you feel like nobody cares, but you're wrong. I wouldn't be here if you were right."

Mariah took in Phil's words. She wanted to believe him. He looked sincere. He sounded sincere, but her entire life, no one had ever told her that she mattered, so why should she believe that anybody would now, especially a complete stranger?

"And I want to listen to whatever it is you have to say," Phil continued. "Anytime, day or night. I will drop what I'm doing and I'll listen."

A tear escaped Mariah's eye, and she quickly and harshly brushed it away. It was as if she was ashamed to let anyone see her shed a tear. "Quit playing with me. Don't try to make it sound like you're saying that because you really care. You're saying that because you get paid to care."

"That's where you're wrong." Julie stepped in. "Dr. Gooden gets paid for a lot of things, but to care is not one of them. He gets a paycheck whether he cares or not. Do you think he's being paid to be here right now? No," Julie answered her own question. "He's here because he cares. I know it's genuine, and I know it's true." She looked Phil in the eyes. "Because I've been on the receiving end before, and I can tell you that this man is the real deal."

Mariah's bottom lip began to tremble; she became so overwhelmed with emotion. She looked as though she wanted to burst at the seams.

"It's all right. Let it out." Phil took back over. "Whatever those tears are for, let them out. Rage, hurt, anger, loneliness . . . it's okay. Let it out."

Mariah fought like hell to keep those tears at bay, but once the dam broke, she lost it, bending over and clutching her belly as if she were in pain.

"It's okay, Mariah," Phil said. He kept saying her name on purpose, so she would know that they knew who she was, that she mattered, and that she was safe. He looked to Julie, and without so much as a signal, they both kneeled down and sat on the floor next to her. Julie put her hand on Mariah's shoulder first, to comfort her, then Phil did the same.

Mariah covered her face with her hands as if she could catch all those tears, but she didn't stand a chance. Phil handed her the pocket square from his suit jacket. She took it and wiped her face.

"Thank you," Mariah whispered as she looked Phil in the eyes. She was doing her best to stop crying, but the harder she tried, the more she cried. "I matter?" she asked, though seeming afraid to hear the answer.

"Yes, you do," Phil said, reaching for her hands. Mariah grabbed onto his hands as if they were life itself, and she shattered like an antique china plate. Mariah leaned her head onto Phil's shoulder and that was it. She sobbed uncontrollably into Phil's chest.

Phil didn't once think about the six-hundred-dollar DKNY suit he was wearing as he was sitting on that filthy floor, with this heartbroken little woman crying on his jacket. He could get another suit, but he didn't want to imagine what might happen if he didn't get through to her.

Julie still had her hand on Mariah's shoulder, but once she finally let go completely, Julie had to get up and compose herself. She wasn't as used to powerfully emotional situations like this one, and she, too, was doing her best not to cry.

Phil looked up at Julie as she was dabbing her tears away. She nodded to him to let him know that she was okay.

"Mariah, can you do something for me, please? I need you to promise me that you will not do what you were thinking about doing. Can you do that for me?"

Mariah pulled her face away from Phil's chest and nodded her head.

"I need to hear you say it."

"Yes," Mariah said softly as she looked at Phil. She caught her breath as she dabbed away the last few tears on her face and slowly stood to her feet. Phil followed suit.

Julie hugged Mariah softly and helped her straighten out her clothes. "I don't want to die," Mariah cried. "I thought I wanted to die, but I don't. I just don't want to feel this way anymore."

Mariah gathered her composure and then pulled away from Julie. She extended her hand to give Julie something.

"What is this?" Julie asked as she accepted the offering. Julie held up the object and read it. It was a bottle of prescription sleeping pills. She looked over at Phil, then back at Mariah. "Can I take these with me?"

Mariah nodded.

Julie looked around. "Do you have any more, or anything else that—"

Mariah cut Julie off. "No," she said, shaking her head. She wiped her nose with her forearm.

"Good. Good," Julie said.

Phil stood watching. He was so relieved that Mariah was alive and well and willing to get some help, not because the court was ordering her to, but because she wanted it.

This moment was bittersweet, though. Fortunately Marc's patient had been saved, but there were no more lifesavers left in the pack for Marc himself.

Phil took Mariah's cell phone and called his own phone with it.

"Now you have my personal number. I meant what I said. If you need me, day or night, call me, and I will be there for you. I give you my word."

Mariah gave Phil a soft smile. "Thank you."

"You gonna be okay here tonight after we leave?"

"Yes," she said as she looked around. "I'll be fine. Probably going to get something to eat and clean up around here a little bit."

"Okay," Phil said as he hugged her.

It caught Mariah off guard, but she didn't mind at all. It was a hug from someone who actually cared about her, so she accepted it without reservation.

"I'll be by here to see you tomorrow," he said.

"I'll see you then," Mariah replied as she turned to hug Julie also. She walked them to the door and let them out.


Outside of Mariah's apartment, Phil and Julie sat in the parked car. Both of them were completely silent, moved by what had just taken place. Julie was deep in thought as she looked down at the bottle of pills.

"Correct me if I'm wrong," Julie spoke, "but did I just witness you save somebody's life?" She looked over at Phil.

"No. *We* just helped save somebody's life." He smiled. "Feels good, doesn't it?"

The corners of Julie's mouth turned up into a smile. "Yes," she said proudly. "Yes, it does."

With the mood now shifted, Phil started the car and drove off.

# Chapter 18

Marc had blown Phil's phone up all night, wanting to know the outcome of his visit with Mariah, but Phil had ignored his best friend's calls. He had to really think about what to do with Marc. This situation could have turned out much worse than it had. Forget about losing jobs and licenses; a life had been at stake.

Sure, Marc had been trying to do all that he could—well, maybe not *all* that he could—but he'd been doing the best that he could, for Marc's own standards anyway. His best hadn't been good enough for Phil, though.

"Julie said you needed to see me." Marc walked through Phil's open door.

Phil had been standing over by the window, staring out, gathering the words he needed to say to his best friend. "Yeah, close the door," Phil said without turning around to look at Marc.

When Marc settled into the seat near Phil's desk, Phil turned around and tossed the bottle of sleeping pills to him.

Marc caught them. "What are these?"

"Those are the pills Mariah Quinton gave to us yesterday. The ones she was going to use to kill herself if we hadn't shown up."

Marc looked at the pill bottle but said nothing.

"I'm gonna have to suspend you, Marc."

"I know, I know," Marc said as if this was now becoming customary. "I know you have to give me some kind of slap on the wrist for the board's sake. I understand."

"No, Marc, you don't get it. I'm suspending you for real this time. Indefinitely. You're suspended, without pay, until I can figure out what's the best way to handle this. And that may mean you losing your job completely."

"Losing my job? Over one incident? An incident that the board doesn't even know about? I mean, yeah, things could have gotten really bad, but they didn't."

Phil couldn't believe his friend's audacity. "Are you kidding me right now? It's not just one incident. We've lost four weekly patients this year, paying patients, and they have all had the same complaint." Phil pointed to Marc. "You! They say you act like you don't care about their circumstances. And you know what? After yesterday, I'm inclined to believe them."

"But that's not true. I do care," Marc argued.

"I can't tell," he said, looking Marc up and down.

"You think you better than me or something? You think just because you know how to get all vulnerable and sensitive with these patients that that makes you more caring than me?" Marc spat. "Who are you to judge me? And who the hell are you to suspend me?"

"I'm the guy who fought to get you this damn job when every other legitimate practice in California turned you down. That's who I am. My investors didn't even want me to hire you in the first place, but I stayed on them because I know what you're capable of, and because I know you are every bit as good a doctor as I am. You just don't act like it. That's who the hell I am. Now, if you'd start being all that you are, then we wouldn't even be having this conversation." By the time Phil finished speaking, he realized he was starting to get loud.

"I don't even know why you trippin' like this," Marc said. "Nothing happened. She didn't take the pills. And guess what? You can take her case."

"I don't need your permission to take her case, and something did happen. You failed a client. What happens next time? If she had killed herself, the state board would have come straight here to get her file. Their first question would have been why didn't we report her severely depressed behavior and recommend medication or something? They'll want to know why we didn't follow up on it. What could I have said? 'Sorry she's dead, but the doctor was taking a damn nap when she was talking about killing herself,'" Phil said mockingly. "We both would have lost our licenses, and if I've told you once, I've told you a million times: I'm not messing up my career because you don't give a damn about yours." Phil was breathing heavily as he tried to restrain his anger so that his voice wouldn't carry out into the lobby.

"Wow. All that from a guy that's burying himself in his work, so he doesn't have to face the fact that his relationship is over. And now what does he do? Once again he takes it out on me."

"It's not like that this time, Marc. It's not about Denise and no game of one-on-one is going to fix this. This conversation is over."

Marc waited for a second, praying that Phil would have a change of heart. When it appeared that Phil was serious about being finished with the conversation, Marc said, "So it's like that?" He raised his hands and let them fall to the side. He collected what was left of his pride and left his best friend's office, not knowing if their friendship would even survive this time.


Phil was straightening his office up when Julie walked in. "Dr. Gooden, your three o'clock is here.

"Thank you," Phil said. "And by the way, would you please fill any open slots I have with as many of Dr. Collins' patients as you can?" Phil sounded so professional and authoritative. It was Dr. Collins and not Marc. This must have been serious, Julie thought.

"You fired him?" Julie asked. She didn't know whether to be shocked or sad. If Phil had fired him, she could certainly understand why, but she knew the caring side of Marc. She'd witnessed it during his altercation with Anthony. No way would he have risked getting hurt or worse if he hadn't cared.

"No, I just suspended him," Phil said, and Julie exhaled softly in relief. "Until I can figure out what to do. Can you send my three o'clock in please?" Phil was done talking about Marc. He had his own patients to tend to, and his load was about to double, so getting behind wasn't an option, or else he'd end up sleeping at his office.

"No problem," Julie said.

"Thank you."

Not even a minute later, Phil's client, Patrice Addison, entered his office. Patrice reminded Phil of Robin Givens in *Boomerang*. Patrice walked in the room with as much sexy as she could muster, which was a lot. She was five feet ten in heels, with long curly hair, a pretty face, and a nice shape. By her own admission, Patrice had a problem controlling her sexual urges. She was a certifiable nymphomaniac, and she wanted and needed sex all the time. She was a woman of means and was financially set, so that had only made her problem easier to feed.

"Ms. Addison, it's good to see you again. Please take a seat," Phil said. "Can I offer you anything?"

Patrice raised her eyebrows. "That depends on what you're offering and how much it's going to cost me." She licked her lips.

"I'm offering bottled water," Phil replied, heading over to the mini fridge in his office. "And trust me; you pay me enough to cover a bottle of water."

"Is that so?"

"Yes, it is. Now, would you like one?"

She shooed her hand and sat down in the chair. "No, thank you. I thought you were offering up something else. Now that, I would have taken." She gave Phil the once over. "And paid for it." She let out a laugh that was a cross between wicked and sexy.

Phil grabbed himself a bottle of water and sat down at his desk. "Patrice, you're pretty aggressive with men. Why do you think that is?" He opened her file.

"I don't know, but I can't control it. It's like there's two of me. There's regular old boring me, then there's this other wild, aggressive woman. She just clicks on and takes over."

Phil took a sip of his water, screwed the cap back on, and then set it on his desk. "Clicks on?" he questioned, picking up his pen to take some notes. "Explain that to me."

Patrice took off her Coach glasses and paused for a second. "I just click on and go after what I want." She stood up. "And right now," she began moving toward Phil, "that's you."

"I'm flattered, Mrs. Addison, I really am." Phil stood up as well. "But I do not get involved with my patients in any way other than professionally."

"Then let's make it professional." Patrice started unbuttoning her shirt. "Dr. Collins has no problem with it. What's your minimum? 'Cause trust me, I got plenty of money. I can make it worth your while."

Phil backed up. "What are you talking about?" He wanted Patrice to keep her shirt on and just get out of there, but he couldn't allow her to leave without explaining what she'd just said about Marc. "The only thing Dr. Collins charges for is therapy sessions."

"And private lap dances," Patrice said, continuing to unbutton her shirt and move toward Phil.

"Private lap dances? In his office?" Phil couldn't believe that Marc was not only having sex with patients, but giving them lap dances—and charging them money on top of that. On second thought, this didn't surprise Phil much, especially in light of the recent developments.

Patrice was now practically chasing Phil around his desk, and while he scooted away from her, he thought about what she had just revealed about Marc. Patients could be a little over the top sometimes, so it was possible this was just a farfetched lie, although he couldn't figure out what her motive would be to tell such a lie. Phil had to talk to Marc personally about this, but first he had to get Patrice dressed and out of there.

"You're unbuttoning your shirt." Phil kept moving away. "Not a good idea." Phil managed to keep the desk between them.

Patrice's D-cups, covered by a black lace bra, fell out of her shirt.

"Oh, no, close that," Phil said, turning his head but still keeping sight of Patrice in his peripheral vision. "If you just keep that closed."

"Shhhhh," Patrice said. She angled the desk so Phil couldn't get by. She then slowly began to untuck his shirt.

"Really, we can't—"

Patrice threw her shirt on Phil's desk and started reaching behind her back to unclasp her bra.

"Do not take that off, Mrs. Addison."

"Call me Patty," she insisted. "As a matter of fact, call me Patty Cake. That's what *Marcus* does."

Patrice threw her bra on Phil's shoulder, and he made a run for the door. He eased out the door, pushing Patrice back in. He snatched his tie from Patrice and closed the door behind him.

Julie stood up from her desk, confusion and concern on her face.

Out of breath and panting, Phil said, "When she changes back into her other personality and gets dressed, get her out of my office please. In the meantime, I'll be in the conference room."

Julie couldn't help but burst out laughing. Phil still had Patrice's bra hanging over his shoulder. He realized it, grabbed it, and set it on Julie's desk. She stopped laughing then.

# Chapter 19

Phil sat at the conference room table gathering his bearings and trying to make sense out of what Patrice had just accused Marc of. The whole thing had him exhausted.

"She's gone." Julie entered the conference room.

"Good," Phil said, not bothering to stand up.

Feeding off of Phil's expression and demeanor, Julie sat down next to him. "You're feeling a little guilty about Marc, aren't you?"

Phil let out a gust of hot air. "Yeah, but what else could I do?"

"I guess just try to get as comfortable as you possibly can between that rock and that hard place," Julie said. "I can understand how you might feel. He's your best friend. But you did the right thing."

"I guess," Phil said, not too convinced.

"You heard from Mariah?"

"Yes, I stopped by on my lunch break to check on her. She had cleaned up her place. She was also looking better, like she had gotten some rest. She asked me to thank you again for being there for her like that. She doesn't have many friends. I told her that she has two new ones now," Phil said with a smile. "Which reminds me." He snapped his finger. "I scheduled an appointment with her. I wrote it down on my calendar, but I need to give it to you so you don't double book me."

"Sounds good," Julie said.

"Anyway, I better get out of here." Phil stood up. "I'ma go grab something to eat." He went to the door.

"Nah, I'm full. Thanks for asking," Julie said sarcastically, rubbing her stomach.

"Oh, my bad." Phil laughed. "Uh, Julie, I'm going to get something to eat if you want to go."

"Well, Dr. Gooden, it's so kind of you to ask just out of the blue." Julie stood. "I think I will."

Phil bowed and extended his hand for her to exit first. When she passed him, he mumbled, "Smart-ass."


"So what's up with you and Anthony?" Phil asked Julie as they sat with their food and drinks at a corner booth in the café style restaurant.

Julie took a sip of her drink. "I haven't started seeing him again, if that's what you mean."

"Well, I'm glad to see that it only took one time for a man to put his hands on you before you were strong enough to leave him."

Julie's eyes cast downward. She took another sip of her drink and allowed her eyes to travel from left to right, anywhere but directly at Phil.

Noticing her reaction, Phil said, "You never really answered my question before. The eye incident: was that the first time he'd put his hands on you?"

Julie slowly removed her mouth from the straw. "Well, yeah, it was. Kinda sorta."

"What's kinda sorta?" Phil asked. "He either hit you before or he didn't."

She leaned back against her seat. "He never really *hit me* hit me before. Things started small," she said. "Him getting in my face and grabbing me, then pushing me and twisting my arm. The bruise you and Marc saw—the black eye—that was only the third time he'd ever left a bruise or mark."

"What do you mean *only?*" Phil questioned. "The first time he got in your face you should have stopped messing with him."

"I know, but he always apologized and promised that it would never happen again."

"They always do." Phil took a sip of his drink. He had to calm himself down. Nothing got under his skin like a man hitting a woman, and he felt himself getting a little upset just talking about it.

Julie looked off past Phil. "I think I just liked having somebody around." She hugged her drink with her hands. "I get lonely." She looked over at Phil to see what type of reaction he'd had to her last comment.

He was still trying to keep things professional between them, so his expression revealed little. He knew that if they stepped even one foot outside of the friend zone, things could either be great or get really messy.

"Look, I'm not about to preach to you or judge you," he said.

"Good," Julie said, "because I've learned my lesson. I don't need anyone beating me up about it."

"And believe me," Phil said, "I don't want anybody beating you period."

Julie tilted her head. "Really?" She sucked her teeth and rolled her eyes.

"I'm serious," Phil said, seeing that Julie was irritated by his slick comment. "Just let me say this: You deserve better than that. You're smart, driven, and beautiful, but I don't think you see all that when you look at yourself. If you did, you wouldn't be dealing with these bums."

Phil's words stung a little, but he was telling the truth. At this moment, it both frustrated Julie and made her angry. "I get that, but then I see women like Denise, who has one of the best men out there, and she just wants to throw him away," Julie ranted. "I mean, if I was your girlfriend . . ." Julie's words trailed off once she realized she was about to speak words that had been hidden in her heart for so long.

Phil just sat there waiting for Julie to finish her thoughts. *Wanting* her to finish her thoughts. The attraction, the energy, the chemistry between them had gone unspoken for so long. Being Julie's superior in the workplace, Phil would have never made the first move or spoken on how he felt about Julie. He never wanted to make her feel as if he was using his power over her in the workplace to get with her. He wanted it to be genuine and to know that it was true reciprocity. That meant Julie speaking on the matter first.

Julie cleared her throat. "Speaking of Denise, and forgive my candor, how long are you going to keep holding on to a relationship that doesn't exist anymore?"

Phil shrugged. He realized that Denise had pretty much been ghost. He hadn't talked to or seen her since she left the ring and disappeared. Funny thing was, Phil actually hadn't thought about her lately. There was the issue with Julie, Shayla and Marc trying to set him up, his parents, his patients, and then dealing with Marc at work. All these things had kept his mind off of Denise. Clearly this had given his heart some time to heal, because now that he sat in front of Julie, it was opened enough to really *see* her.

"Good question," Phil answered Julie, but she could tell that his entire attitude had shifted upon the mention of Denise's name.

"We don't have to talk about her."

"Good."

"So, what's on your agenda this evening?" Julie asked, changing the subject. "Let me guess. You're going home and bury yourself in some work tonight, right?"

Phil had just heard Marc accuse him of burying himself in work. With Julie saying the same thing, Phil realized that maybe Marc's words were more than just spiteful rhetoric Maybe there was some truth to it.

"Actually, I am going to fix myself a drink, turn on Netflix, chill, and kick my feet up." Phil decided at the spur of the moment.

Julie sat there with a look in her eyes that said, "I wanna go." It was obvious she was waiting for an invitation.

Phil smiled. "You're welcome to join me." It hit him just then that he'd practically asked Julie out on what could be considered a date. He looked down at his watch. "Let's get out of here," he suggested, trying to hide the nervousness that was building inside of him. Not only would it be a date, but it would be their first date . . . at his house!

"Check, please!" He had to get out of there before she accepted, because Lord only knew what it could turn into after that.

# Chapter 20

"Thank you for letting me join you," Julie said as she sat down on Phil's couch. She leaned forward and grabbed a handful of popcorn from the bowl on the table next to the remote control. "What's playing on the big screen? A horror movie? Sci-fi thriller?" Julie stared at Phil for a moment, sizing him up. "Nah, you look like an action movie kind of man."

Phil stood there watching Julie talk non-stop while stuffing her face with popcorn in between. He didn't reply.

"What's wrong?" Julie asked.

"Oh, nothing," Phil said. "Just waiting for you to get everything out of your system so that we can enjoy a nice, comfortable and relaxing evening. Just two friends enjoying a movie, nothing more and nothing less."

Julie exhaled. "It's that obvious, huh?"

"Uh, yeah," Phil said then started walking to his kitchen. "I'm going to grab us something to drink. You okay with red wine?"

"I am very okay with that," Julie said with a smile.

"Be right back." Phil entered the kitchen and let out a huge gust of wind. Although he'd played it cool, calm, and collected, he was just as nervous as Julie. He didn't know what to make of the two of them spending an evening together alone in his house.

As he gathered their drinks, he thought about it and decided he'd look at it the same way he'd told Julie to:

They were just two friends enjoying a movie. He'd try to forget about the fact that there was a huge attraction that existed between them. When he returned to the living room to see that Julie had taken off her sweater, he didn't know if that attraction would be possible to ignore.

Julie had kicked off her shoes and had her feet up under her. Her legs looked so long and slender in that midnight blue pencil skirt that he could hardly keep his eyes off of them.

"Oooh, Cherry Coke and Twizzlers," Julie said when she saw Phil return. "You know that's my favorite."

"There hasn't been a day that's gone by at work where I didn't see a can sitting on your desk." Phil winked as he doubled back to the kitchen to grab the wine he had poured for them.

"Very observant," Julie said.

"I try to be," Phil said, sitting down next to Julie. "After all, my patients expect me to be."

"But I'm not one of your patients," Julie was quick to say.

Phil looked at Julie. "Yeah, you're right about that."

"So, tell me, what are some of the other things you notice about me?"

Phil sipped his drink and looked at Julie. "You serious?" he asked.

"Yeah. Then I'll tell you some things about you," Julie said, excitedly turning from the television to face Phil. "But you go first."

Phil thought for a moment. He set his drink on the table and then faced Julie. "You're favorite drink is Cherry Coke; that I've confirmed. You love Chinese food, Twizzlers, and Tupac. Your favorite color is red, which does happen to look amazing on you—like any color does."

Julie did her best to fight back her smile, but it hadn't worked. He had even been able to make her blush a little.

"I know quite a bit about you."

"Likewise," she said.

"Really?"

"Oh, you'd be amazed at how much I know about you," Julie teased.

Phil said seriously. "Do tell."

Two hours went by, and Phil still hadn't scrolled through Netflix to the movie they were supposed to watch. Instead they talked, laughed, emptied that first bottle of red wine and were working on a second.

Phil was right in the middle of telling Julie about the first fight he got into as a child when he heard a soft snoring sound. He looked over to see Julie sound asleep. Before he could even say anything, her head slumped over onto his shoulder. He liked her being that close.

Phil smiled and then slowly eased up into a standing position, with Julie in his arms. He lifted her and began carrying her to his bedroom.

"What's going on?" a discombobulated Julie asked as she woke up in Phil's arms.

"You're tired," Phil said in a whisper. "Either you're tired or I'm boring. You fell asleep on me."

Julie looked around as they entered Phil's bedroom. "Oh, I'm sorry." She slithered out of his arms just as he'd arrived at his bed. "I better head home."

"Oh, no, it's okay," Phil said. "I'll take the couch. Besides, you've had too many glasses of wine to drive." He chuckled.

"You're so silly." Julie gave Phil a soft and playful slap on his chest. She allowed it to rest there as she stared in Phil's eyes. When she went to pull her hand away, Phil grabbed it, then lifted it to his mouth and kissed the palm of her hand. He kissed the back of her hand, then looked at her for a reaction. The expression on her face welcomed the kiss. One by one, Phil began placing each of Julie's fingers to his mouth. He planted soft, pliant kisses on each of them.

Julie's eyelids fell closed as she took in Phil's touch.

Once he was done with that hand, he took Julie's other hand in his and did a repeat. Next it was her lips. Before Phil knew it, Julie had wrapped her arms around his neck and was kissing him back deeply.

No words were spoken, just action, as Phil lifted Julie onto his bed and laid her down. He slowly undressed her, planting kisses all over her body.

"Turn over." Phil's voice traveled through the darkness.

Julie did as she was told, accepting kisses from Phil all down her back, his tongue rolling across her sexy, chocolate backside, then down the back of her legs. Chill bumps covered her, but within moments, Phil's body was what covered her, as he entered her from the back. She inhaled quickly and held on for the ride.

Julie gripped the sheets as Phil slid in and out of her. They spoke no words. Their breathing and her moans made for an incredible duet. It was the sweetest music. She was speechless. Phil felt so good inside of her. She feared that if she did in fact speak, her voice would break and she would cry.

Phil wrapped his hands over hers. She gripped the sheets, while he gripped her hands.

Trying to be quiet was no longer an option for Julie, as louder moans of pleasure escaped her mouth. Phil echoed her, as slowly but surely, they reached climax together.


The next morning dawned beautifully as the sun peeked in through the blinds after their night of passion. Phil was lying on his back, while Julie slept on his chest.

Phil breathed deeply, which pulled Julie out of her slumber. She opened her eyes and then slowly looked around, realizing that she was not at home in her bedroom. She looked down to see her hand planted on a man's chest, and then looked up to see Phil sound asleep. She laid her head back on his chest and closed her eyes as a slight smile spread across her lips.

That was when everything hit her. She jumped up off his chest, clenching the sheet to her chest. "Dr. Gooden?"

Phil was startled awake after having both the warmth of Julie's body and the sheet ripped from him. "Julie?" he said groggily.

"Dr. Gooden." Julie held the sheet even tighter in embarrassment. "Did we . . .?"

Phil had a serious look on his face as he thought for a minute. He started to remember last night's events. The corners of his mouth turned up. "Yeah, we did. Right here in this bed." He then began pointing around the room. "And over here, and on the chair, and on the wall right here."

"Uggh!" Julie buried her face in her hands. She had slept with Phil on their first date that really wasn't a date. And he was her boss!

An uncomfortable silence fell over the room for a second.

"So what do we do now?" Julie asked.

"What is there to do? We were safe. We're both grown and single."

"But isn't this unethical or something?"

"Unethical?" Phil laughed. "You're not a patient, Julie."

"But you're my boss." She turned and looked at Phil.

"Is this going to change anything at work?" he asked.

"No, not at all. But this can't happen again. Not like this."

Phil had bedded Julie with absolutely no understanding of what the two of them had going on. His issue with Denise was that the two of them weren't on the same page. Now he didn't even know if he and Julie were reading the same book.

"I agree," Phil replied.

Julie began looking around. She spotted a clock on the nightstand on Phil's side of the bed, but she couldn't see the face of it. "What time is it?"

Phil looked over at the clock. "Seven."

"Your first appointment today is—"

"At ten."

There was a pregnant pause. Julie and Phil slowly turned to face each other. If they could have read each other's minds, they would have found that they'd been thinking the same thing. Phil gave Julie a flirtatious smirk, and she returned it back to him.

"We got time?" Julie asked.

"Yeah," Phil said as he rolled over and licked his lips, eager to taste Julie. Like they say: breakfast is the most important meal of the day.

# Chapter 21

"I haven't seen you in three weeks, Mr. Egan. What's been going on?" Phil asked his patient.

"I didn't feel much like having a session." Mr. Egan shrugged. He wasn't in the happy-go-lucky mood Phil was used to seeing him in.

"Mind if I ask why?"

"My wife caught me cheating."

"What exactly do you mean *caught*?" Phil wanted specifics in order to be able to evaluate the situation properly.

"Evidently, she overheard me talking to a female associate making plans to meet up. When I left the house, she followed me and caught me making out with the woman in my truck."

"You said you were really going to work on the cheating."

"I did. We said a week, remember? I made it an entire week." He stared off, shaking his head. "But that eighth day..."

This was a bittersweet moment for Phil. He was proud that Mr. Egan had made it a whole seven days without being unfaithful. He was disappointed, though, that he hadn't challenged him to a month.

"What did she do?" Phil asked, preparing himself for the awful details.

Mr. Egan took out his phone. "She took a picture with her cell." He handed the phone to Phil. "She took a picture with her cell phone and then sent it to me."

"And you?" Phil asked as he took the phone.

"Hell, I denied it, of course."

Phil looked down at the picture on the phone. He turned his head sideways and then turned the phone upside down. "You denied this?" He looked up at his patient and handed him his phone. "Mr. Egan, your wife isn't blind. You can't deny this," Phil said sarcastically.

"I just told her it wasn't me."

"She left, didn't she?"

"Yes," Mr. Egan said in a depressed tone.

Phil felt bad for Mr. Egan. He was clearly disappointed that he had let his wife and Phil down again. On top of that, he had hurt his wife badly this time. Knowing that a person's mate is cheating on them is bad, but seeing it in person had to be hell, Phil thought. Phil knew he had to help Mr. Egan somehow.

"You know what you have to do, don't you?" Phil asked. "You have to admit that it was you."

"Oh, hell no!" Mr. Egan said, shooting straight up and shaking his head adamantly.

Phil was doing just the opposite, nodding emphatically. "Yes. That's the only shot you have at saving your marriage, Mr. Egan. Obviously you still love her, or you wouldn't be here trying to find out what to do. Right?"

"Right."

"Then listen up," Phil said. "Three things." He rested his elbow on his desk as he held up his fist. "You have to 'fess up and admit what you did." He popped up his index finger. "You have to suggest and commit to marital counseling *with* your wife." He held up his middle finger as well. "And you have to stop cheating!" His ring finger joined the other two. "Keep it in your pants, unless your wife's around. Okay?"

"Okay," Mr. Egan agreed. "But for how many weeks?"

Phil shot him a threatening look.

"Okay. I said okay," Mr. Egan reiterated.

"You know exactly what you have to do, so do it, or this is going to be our last session."

"But I'm paying you."

"It's not about the money, Mr. Egan. I am not going to keep trying to fix this if you're not going to try with me. It's not my marriage; it's yours. I could be using this time to help someone who at least is going to put forth a genuine effort. Do we understand each other?"

"I hear you, Doc," Mr. Egan said. "And I'm going to give it a genuine try this time. I can't lose my wife."

Phil wanted to truly believe his patient this time, but his gut told him that this may be the last time he saw Mr. Egan.

"I'm not used to this, being out here at this time of day," Phil said to Julie as the two of them were walking with the nice cityscape behind them. "My head is usually buried in a file."

"What about the times you're with your one patient?" Julie asked. "You know, the one in the wheelchair who likes to have his sessions outside."

"Oh, yeah, Mr. Sallinger," Phil said. "Yeah, but usually I'm tuned in to what he's saying."

"Too tuned in to notice all of God's lovely creations around you?"

Phil thought for a minute. "Yeah, pretty much."

Julie shook her head. "You've got to learn to live a little, boss."

Phil realized that although he and Denise had shared some exotic and romantic trips together and had had more mind-blowing sex encounters than he could count, they'd never done something as simple as just take a walk and enjoy life.

Phil looked to Julie. "Yeah, maybe you're right."

"A man who's not afraid to admit when a woman is right. I like that." She let out a little laugh. Phil had never noticed how cute her laugh was.

There was a lot he was starting to notice about his secretary. His friend. He was seriously considering making her more than just those things, but before they started heading down the same road that had ended up with him and Denise going in different directions, he decided they needed to talk.

The energy had been a little weird between him and Julie while in the workplace. The last thing he wanted was for things to change between them for the worse.

"We should talk about the other night," Phil said.

Julie exhaled like she had known this moment was coming. "Look, truthfully, I needed that . . . because hitting on me was the only thing Anthony was good at. So it's cool."

"I was kind of worried that you wouldn't be able to keep business and personal separate. I'm glad I was wrong."

"Not so fast." Julie stopped walking. "There is one issue."

*I knew it,* Phil thought as he stopped walking.

"The things that we did . . ." Julie paused, which made Phil's heart race with worry. "I might need that again. Soon." Julie started walking again. She'd spoken, and her word was bond.

"How soon?" Phil asked with a raised eyebrow.

Julie looked around and saw a little trail off to the left, covered with trees. "No time like the present." She grabbed Phil by the hand, and they disappeared along the trail.


After their brief, yet exhilarating, quickie on the trail, Phil and Julie returned to his house. Their adrenaline was still on ten as they entered the door, kissing and undressing. They closed the door behind them and continued through the living room.

Suddenly, Phil stopped. "Wait. I want to make sure we're clear about this. We are just two single people enjoying each other's company." Phil didn't want to have the wrong idea about this. He couldn't take the chance of wanting to spend the rest of his life with a woman and her not wanting the same in return. For now, this would be only about friendship and mind-blowing sex. No expectations. No heartbreak. He definitely didn't want to hurt Julie's feelings.

"I'm fine with that," Julie agreed without much thought. She was too hot and bothered to take it all in mentally right now. "Now, if you're done talking, can you please grab a condom and give me what I need?"

Turned on by Julie's request, Phil picked her up. She wrapped her legs around his waist as he carried her to the bedroom.

Everything happened so quickly that it was like a montage of shots in an X-rated film. One minute Phil was laying Julie on the floor as he continued to kiss her. The next minute, she was clenching his back muscles, digging in deep. Finally, they were against the wall, their hands interlocked as they reached the mountain's peak together. They looked more like lovers than just friends. They looked like more than just two single people enjoying each other's company. They looked like a couple in love, though they weren't. For now, they were more like a couple falling in love. What they didn't realize at the time was that there were still some loose ends that needed to be taken care of or else things would surely unravel.

# Chapter 22

Phil's schedule had been so jam-packed that getting Mariah in for some office time had been next to impossible. By the time he remembered to give Julie the date he'd scheduled on his own to see Mariah, Julie had already booked that slot, so he had to cancel with Mariah. Still, he knew he needed to check on her.

As he approached her place, he hoped it wasn't too late to be showing up on her doorstep. He wished he'd thought to call her first, but her file with her phone number in it was back at the office.

As Phil walked up the driveway to Mariah's house, he heard a familiar voice. It wasn't Mariah's voice either, but a male's voice instead. Phil stood off to the side of the porch where he couldn't be seen. He didn't want to cause any confusion.

"Thanks again for coming by to check on me, Dr. Collins," Mariah said.

"You're welcome," Marc replied, stepping out onto the porch. "I'll call first, but I'll be by again in a couple days. See you then."

Phil stayed hidden off to the side. He waited a few minutes, until he saw Marc's car drive by. Given Marc's track record for seducing patients, the thought crossed Phil's mind that maybe his friend's reason for visiting hadn't been so innocent. The thought that entered his mind made his stomach turn.

"His ass better not be . . ." His words trailed off as he hustled to Mariah's door and knocked. If Marc was trying to take advantage of this woman's fragile mental state, then not only would he fire Marc himself, but he'd see to it that he never treated another patient for as long as he lived—on top of giving him a well-deserved ass whipping. Friend or not, Phil had taken an oath to care for his patients, even if that meant at the expense of a friendship.

"Did you forget something, Dr. Coll—" Mariah stopped abruptly once she saw that it was Phil at her door and not Marc. "Hey, Dr. Gooden, how are you doing?" She was letting off some nervous energy that didn't go undetected by Phil.

"I'm not sure yet," Phil said then got right to the point. "You didn't tell me that Dr. Collins had contacted you."

Mariah stammered a little. "He made me promise not to."

"How long has he been coming by here?"

Mariah tried to shrug it off and downplay it. "A couple weeks. We talk for hours sometimes." She smiled as she looked off and nodded. "You know, he's a really good listener after all." She looked at Phil. "I hope he changes his mind."

"About what?" Phil inquired.

"He said something about changing careers?"

Phil thought for a moment. He'd never heard Marc mention anything about a change in careers. Perhaps he was referring to the possibility that he thought he might have lost his job.

"I wouldn't worry about that if I were you. You just keep getting better. Deal?"

"Deal," Mariah agreed.

There was a light behind her eyes now where there had once been darkness. She appeared to genuinely be improving. She wanted this help. She wanted to do better. Phil couldn't question that. Mariah was the exact patient Phil was referring to when he told Mr. Egan that there were other patients who could be using his time slot. Unbeknownst to Phil, though, it looked as though Marc had her covered the entire time.

Phil was pleased that for once Marc seemed to be thinking about someone other than himself; however, that still didn't change the fact that he was suspended and technically, or legally, wasn't supposed to be practicing. This was something Phil had to address now.

Phil hoped Marc had decided to go home and not over to Shayla's as he walked up to Marc's door and knocked. A few seconds later, Marc came and opened the door.

"You got a minute?" Phil asked.

Marc opened the door and stepped aside to allow Phil to enter. "Yeah, come on in."

Phil walked in with his hands in his pockets.

"You want something to drink?" Marc offered.

"Nah."

Marc went and sat down. Phil followed his lead and did the same.

"I'm starting to think that I made the wrong decision," Phil started.

Marc sighed. "I already know where this is going."

"No, I don't think you do," Phil said.

"You were right," Marc continued. "That girl could have died, and I would have had to carry that mess with me for the rest of my life." Marc nodded his head. "You did the right thing."

Phil was surprised by what Marc was saying, but he remained quiet to hear him out.

"I got it good, man. I got a job where I get to help people change their lives for the better every day. I'm thirty with no kids, and I can make six figures and live good. I just need to make better decisions, grow the hell up, and start paying attention to what matters most, which is life." He looked at Phil. "And friends who look out for me."

Phil nodded in agreement.

"And here I am about to blow everything," Marc said, sounding more angry at himself than Phil had ever been. "Look, I'm not promising to be perfect, but I can and will be the professional you need me to be. I know you've heard this song and dance before, but now it's to a different beat, and I mean it this time."

Phil thought for a moment. He looked at Marc. "No more careless behavior with your patients?"

"No more," Marc affirmed.

"No more coming to work with a hangover?"

"No more."

"No more sex with your patients?"

Marc raised an eyebrow. "I'll get back with you on that one."

Phil shot Marc a stern look.

"All right, all right," Marc finally agreed.

"Even after business hours?" Phil wanted complete clarity.

"No more."

"Speaking of which, I have to ask this," Phil said. "You weren't sleeping with Mariah, were y—"

"No!" Marc was quick to say with a tone of offense.

"I had to ask," Phil said. "She told me you'd been stopping by to see her."

"You have my word on it," Marc assured him. "Besides, I'm already in the doghouse with Shayla."

"She caught you?" Phil inquired.

"Nah. I just got tired of trying to remember all my lies. It was too much work. I told her I was seeing other people. She was hurt because she thought we were exclusive. We might be able to work it out. I'll just have to wait and see, but right now I have to get my life together." Marc put his hands behind his head and leaned back against the couch.

"Shayla's a nice girl. She seems like the forgiving type," Phil said, trying to give his best friend hope. "Either way, it'll be good to have you back. I can't wait to give all your crazy-ass patients back to you."

"So it's official? I'm off suspension?"

"You're off suspension."

"Yes!" Marc said, standing up and pumping his fist in the air. "Hey. Did you mean what you said about me being as good a doctor as you?"

Phil frowned while he looked off in thought. Then he relaxed into a laugh. "All day, man. All day."

They gave each other dap.

"Thanks, man."

# Chapter 23

The next morning, Marc entered his office and looked around, glad to be back. He immediately sat down and dove into work. He wasn't on YouTube or checking his social media pages. He was actually reading through files and taking notes. He had taken down the baseball glove that was hanging on the wall, then swept, mopped, and dusted. He'd found some nicer chairs, and an extra area rug in another unused office. It had definitely helped give his office a warmer feel, which would suffice until the new furniture he had ordered arrived. One thing he hadn't done was take down that expired cat calendar, and he didn't plan to. It gave the office character, and it was a conversation starter for all those who saw it. Marc did, however, order a couple nice paintings to hang next to the calendar.

When his first patient for the day arrived, he was fully attentive. Unlike Phil, he usually did more talking than listening, but in the case with this patient, Brenda Oliver, he didn't have a choice. Brenda was talking a hundred miles a minute, and Marc could barely get a word in edgewise.

"And at first, I thought it was me and something I was doing, but then I thought no, it can't be me or anything I'm doing, because I haven't done anything wrong, you know?"

"Well, it might—"

"So then I figured that it must be something else. If it's not me, then what is it? It's gotta be something, because he is always frustrated with me. Every single time we sit down to talk about something, it always starts off good, but just like clockwork, about halfway through the conversation, Marty always gets an attitude, or gets frustrated and blows up."

"It might have something to do—"

"It's communication. The communication in our marriage is missing. It's completely non-existent. I just think—"

It was Marc's turn to cut her off. "No, Mrs. Oliver, it's not. But because you talk enough for three people, your husband probably can't even get a word in, and he gets frustrated, just like I am now!" Realizing his voice had risen with each word, Marc relaxed and started counting backward from ten.

"What exactly are you saying, Doctor?" Brenda took offense.

*Four, three, two, one.* Marc finished his countdown and then spoke. "This is going to sound harsh, but you talk too much, and you don't listen enough. That's why your husband gets mad when you sit down to talk about important family issues. Communication involves talking *and* listening, Mrs. Oliver. You got the talking part down. Now you need to work on your listening."

A lightbulb went off in Marc's head. Perhaps the message he'd just spoken to Brenda had actually been for him. Like they say: The message is always for the messenger first.

Brenda looked as though she was accepting of what Marc had just said to her, which was the truth, and now she was willing to do something about it. "Well, what do you suggest?"

"You see what you just did? You asked me a question and waited for my answer. Do that with your husband. Let him finish what he is saying before you start talking again. And by you taking that position, he can follow suit and let you finish your statements before he starts. It's like dancing. A good conversation between two people is like a dance. Ballroom, or salsa: there's interaction, there's a rhythm and a flow. In your conversations with your husband, you're like a stripper." He cleared his throat. "You're the only one dancing."

Brenda nodded. "I think I get the point."

"Good."

"But sometimes he'll sit and won't say anything, and I feel like I should say something."

"Let me let you in on a secret," Marc said. "Give a man a comfortable chair and a beer, and he can sit there for hours without saying a word. It doesn't mean that he is upset; it means he needs some peace and quiet. As men, we're just built that way. Give your husband his space sometimes, and he will thank you for it. And it will cut down on the arguments."

Mrs. Oliver's eyes lit up, possibly because she had seen some light at the end of her talkative tunnel.

"So between today and our next appointment, you're going to . . ." He pointed to Brenda, letting her know that it was her turn to talk.

"Listen more."

"And . . ."

"Talk a little less."

"And lastly . . ."

"Give Marty some space."

"You've got it," Marc said.

Brenda left his office happy and proud. Marc was happy and proud too—happy to be back at work helping others, and proud that he hadn't put in his earbuds during Brenda's session.

"Whew," Marc said when he sat back down at his desk after showing Brenda out. He felt like he needed a nap after that session, but he realized that he had another patient coming in an hour. He grabbed the casefile for his next appointment and started planning the strategy and session points. That nap was going to have to wait. He had dreams that were worth more than his sleep.


"Dr. Gooden, you have a visitor," Julie said over the intercom. Usually when she announced a patient she sounded perky. This time there was a hint of annoyance in her tone.

"Okay, send them in," Phil replied.

A couple seconds later, Phil sensed someone enter his office and he looked up. It was safe to say that he'd not been expecting this visitor. Neither had Julie, which explained her tone.

"Surprised to see me?"

Phil stood from his desk, still somewhat shocked. "Actually, I am."

Denise took a few steps inside the room.

"I told myself I was going to give you space," she said. "That I was going to let you take lead. But you've been on my mind lately, so I wanted to come by and see you."

"What's wrong? Trouble in paradise? You and your ball player having problems?" Phil asked with disdain.

Denise's eyes grew as wide as saucers, but then she tried to play it off by straightening up her facial expression.

"What, you didn't think I knew? It doesn't matter anyway. I'm working." He sat back down.

Denise knew she was busted, but what could she say about it that would change things? Nothing. So, that's what she did. She left that subject in the dust and moved on with another.

"Jealous. Does that mean you still think about me? Still want me? If you can't have me, no one can?" Denise teased and taunted sensually as she stepped toward Phil's desk.

Phil kept working. He did not want to show her that she was getting a rise out of him.

"Do you still love me?" she asked.

Phil said nothing out loud, but in his head he was reprimanding himself for being so weak for allowing Denise's presence, her voice, her scent to get to him.

"Why won't you look at me?

He wanted to look badly, feeling the urge to take her in visually, but he resisted. He could tell that it irked her that he wouldn't, but Phil also knew that it took away some of her power. Speak no evil, see no evil: Phil would say very little, and see even less.

"Do you still have the ring? Because I've been thinking that maybe, just maybe, you've been right about our relationship all along. In this time we've been apart, I've gotten the opportunity to see that the grass isn't always greener."

*Yeah, right. I bet she has,* he said to himself.

"Don't act like you've been Mr. Perfect while we've been apart," Denise said, clearly thrown off her game by his silence.

Phil had the same look on his face that Denise had when he busted her.

"Mm-hmm. Didn't know I knew about you and your little secretary out there, now, did you?" Denise said. "I saw you two that day leaving the café all hugged up. Not to mention the way she glared at me when I got here today. But I'm not mad. You know and I know that no one else can fill the void we left in each other's lives, right?"

Phil swallowed hard but still said nothing. He felt that not engaging with her would keep him strong.

"It's okay. You don't have to say anything. I know the answer," Denise said.

After a few more seconds of silence, she said, "Well, I won't keep you. You've got my number when you're ready to talk." She kissed Phil on the cheek and then left Phil sitting there to think about everything she'd said.

He looked over at the chessboard, at his and Mr. Adams' unfinished game. That pretty much mirrored his and Denise's relationship.

# Chapter 24

Phil was still thinking later that evening as he lay in bed next to Julie at his place. Phil was so out of it that he hadn't even realized Julie had been staring at him for a full minute.

"You still love her, don't you?" Julie asked.

Her voice was what finally snapped Phil out of his daze. "Huh? What?" He turned to look at Julie.

"Denise. You still love her, don't you?"

Phil turned to look forward.

"You haven't said a word about her coming to see you today. I figure she's what's on your mind. I guess I only hope she wasn't on your mind when we—"

Phil quickly turned to face Julie again. "Oh God, no, Julie. Never." He shook his head.

Julie exhaled. "Good," she said, relieved. "You still didn't answer my question, though. Do you still love her?"

Phil exhaled. "I don't know."

"Sure wish you would have told me that in the beginning."

Phil rolled on his side to face her. "I told you that I wasn't ready for a relationship, and we agreed, no complications. Friends with benefits. Remember that conversation?"

"Friends with benefits?" Julie snapped. "I don't remember those words being used."

"Two single people, enjoying each other's company. No expectations. Remember those words? It all means the same no matter what words you use," Phil said.

Julie folded her arms and began shaking her head. "I'm sorry. I can't do this. I can't spend the kind of time we spend and make the kind of love we make and not have feelings for you. You mean to tell me that you have no feelings for me at all?"

"I didn't say I didn't have feelings for you."

"Well, do you?"

"I don't know what I feel, Julie. I can help fix everybody's problems except mine," Phil finally admitted out loud. He'd been feeling that way for a while. "I don't know!" He slammed his hands down on the bed beside him in aggravation.

Julie jumped up out of the bed and began gathering her things. "Well, I'm going to let you figure it out."

"You don't have to leave."

"Yeah, but I think I should," Julie said as she walked out of the bedroom with an armful of clothes.

"Damn it!" Phil said. He had to get it together. If he didn't, he just might find himself alone for the rest of his life. Or even worse, he could end up like Marc. He shuddered at the thought.

Phil and Marc were sitting in the café, and Marc was shaking his head at all his best friend had caught him up on regarding him and Julie.

"That explains why Julie called off from work today. I don't think she even called off work when her momma died," Marc said.

"Man, shut up," Phil said. "Her momma is alive and well. Lives over there off of Pico and LaCienega." Phil exhaled. "But I don't think Julie's coming back. It's cool, though. I'm not going to get in a relationship again until I am ready to be in one. I made that crystal clear to her from day one, and she still caught feelings, and now I'm the villain. Women say one thing but mean another."

Marc let out a chuckle. "You know how it goes with women. When you're right, you're wrong; when you're wrong, you're wrong; and when you don't know . . . you're still wrong."

Phil was ready to change the subject away from him and Julie. "So what's up with you and Shayla?"

"Ughh, I'm in the same boat you're in. Trying to figure what the hell to do." Marc sucked his teeth and tried to put the subject back on Phil. "So, what's the deal with you and Denise then? I mean, it sounds like she's ready to give you what you want, so what's the problem?"

"I don't know," Phil said. "It just confused the hell out of things. It seemed like Julie and I had this understanding. Denise had been out of sight and out of mind, but then she waltzes through that door and messes everything up, mainly my head."

"You mean *you* messed everything up."

Phil couldn't deny Marc's correction. "Yeah, exactly."

"You can do one of two things. You can let Denise come back, which would be stupid, 'cause she's just gonna do it again the next time she runs into somebody with more money than you, a little bit taller than you. . . . I don't know, maybe just more handsome than you, depending on whether you're into a five o'clock shadow thing like ol' boy she was with. He did have a great beard."

"Marc!"

"Beards are the new six-pack."

"I can't with you."

"Okay, okay, but seriously. The one other thing you can do is permanently close the door with Denise and roll the dice with Julie."

Phil thought for a minute. "I know hell is freezing over now."

"Why?" Marc asked.

"Because I'm actually about to take some advice from you."

Marc smiled proudly. It wasn't every day people actually took his advice. First Brenda and now Phil. He was on a roll. The question was, though, just which piece of Marc's advice would Phil take?

# Chapter 25

Julie was sitting on her couch eating ice cream right out of the carton when there was a knock at the door. She looked up from the television but opted not to answer the door. Wasn't it an unofficial rule that if the person didn't call before they came, then technically you didn't have to answer the door, even if they could hear the television on inside?

After the second knock, followed by a third, Julie decided to answer the door or else she'd never get to enjoy her ice cream and this episode of *Snapped* in peace. She was so bummed out after her breakup with Phil the night before that she didn't even bother to check to see who was at the door. It didn't matter. Whoever it was would get a cussing out. She just flung it open and threw her hands on her hips with an attitude to fuss out whoever the unannounced visitor was.

Julie opened her mouth to speak, but there was nothing to say to this person, so she hurriedly went to slam the door closed.

"Julie, wait!" he said, sticking his foot in the door to keep it from closing all the way.

"No. Go away or else I'll call the police."

"Wait a minute. I just want to talk."

"I'm listening," Julie said, still trying to close the door.

"There was no excuse for me putting my hands on you," Anthony said. "I'm sorry. I know it's too little too late, but I'm getting some help for my problem. This was my fault, not yours, and I hope that one day you can forgive me. That's all I wanted to say."

"Thank you," Julie said. Anthony sounded so textbook. Even if he was telling the truth and meant his apology from the bottom of his heart, he was not coming inside her house.

"You're welcome. And please, don't tell your friends from work that I stopped by. I'm just now healing up, and—"

Julie smiled as the beat-down replayed in her mind. "I won't," she said.

Anthony paused, probably hoping Julie would let him in. It didn't take him long to realize that wasn't going to happen.

"Okay, then," he said. "I guess I'll see you around."

He stepped away from the door, and Julie slammed it closed in his face and locked it. She had no problem forgiving him, as long as it was from the other side of that door.

"Stop bickering, please," Marc pleaded with Mr. and Mrs. Walker. After the cussing out he'd given them last time, he was surprised the pair had come back for more. "Look, you two obviously can't stand each other, but you wouldn't be here trying to work this out if you didn't love one another. Am I right?"

"Yes," Mr. Walker said.

"Yes," Mrs. Walker confirmed.

"Okay," Marc said, directing his attention to Mr. Walker. "Tell your wife something nice that's true to your wife."

Mr. Walker looked at his wife and paused. "I like the way your butt looks in that outfit."

It wasn't exactly the romantic statement that Marc was hoping for, but if it put a smile on Mrs. Walker's face, then it was good enough.

Mrs. Walker's eyes lit up. "Really?"

Mr. Walker leaned back and did a double take of his wife's behind. "Yeah."

Mrs. Walker blushed.

"Now you," Marc said to Mrs. Walker.

Mrs. Walker looked at her husband. "I think you're sexy when you're angry."

Mr. Walker pulled his neck back, stunned. "Is that why you're always nit-picking at me, so you can piss me off?"

Mrs. Walker chuckled. "Yes, but it always backfires. When you're mad at me, you never wanna have make-up sex, and that's the whole point of me trying to make you mad."

Marc intervened, reaching his hand out toward them as if he were pressing a button on a remote. "Pause."

The Walkers both looked at him like he was crazy.

"Have you thought about skipping the argument and going straight to the make-up sex?" he said to Mrs. Walker.

"No," Mrs. Walker replied.

"That's a great place to start. For that matter, you can both pretend to be mad at each other, and then skip straight to the good part. Secondly," Marc continued, directing his words at Mrs. Walker. "You. Stop nagging your husband. If you want some attention, say, 'Baby, I need some attention.'" He spoke to Mr. Walker next. "And you. That is the love of your life." He pointed to Mrs. Walker. "Stop talking to her the way you have been. She's going to follow your lead. No matter how mad you are at her during an argument, if you don't curse at her or raise your voice at her, she's going to do the same. Am I right, Mrs. Walker?"

Mrs. Walker mumbled something under her breath.

"Right, Mrs. Walker?" Marc repeated.

"Yes," she replied, loud and clear this time.

Marc sat back and directed his next statement to the couple. "Are you going to be alone at home today?"

"For a few hours," Mrs. Walker answered.

"Good. This is what I want you to do," Marc said to Mr. Walker. "When you walk in the door, I want you to set her on the kitchen table and take it."

"Oh, my," Mrs. Walker said, clutching her proverbial pearls.

"I want you to have vigorous, aggressive make-up sex, without the argument. Can you do that?"

Mr. Walker nodded. "Yes."

"And not just today. I want you to have as much sex as possible between now and next week. I mean, for no reason at all. Just do it, dammit." He turned to Mrs. Walker. "And you. All the time you used to spend thinking of things to nag about, I want you to use that time to find sexy outfits to wear for him. And different fruit toppings to cover yourself in, so he can lick them off. Do thoughtful things that you know the man you love will appreciate. Okay?"

"Okay," Mrs. Walker replied, looking eager to follow her therapist's instructions. She looked to her husband, nodding. He began nodding in agreement.

They both turned to Marc, who said, "Mr. Walker, this woman is your Michelle Obama, your Beyoncé, and everything in between. Treat her accordingly. If you make her feel like the First Lady, she will make you feel like the President."

Mr. Walker looked lovingly over at his wife, thinking about the things Marc was saying. "I can handle that."

Marc looked from one to the other with a questioning look. "Why are you still here? There's make-up sex waiting for you at home."

The couple jumped up out of their seats, nearly stumbling over one another.

"He has a good point, dear," Mr. Walker said, leading the way.

"Right behind you, honey," Mrs. Walker said, following her husband out the door.

Mr. Walker stopped halfway to the door and let his wife go in front of him. "Ladies first, First Lady," he said with a huge smile. Mrs. Walker grinned wide and walked out as Mr. Walker gave her a flirtatious smack on the ass. Then they were gone.

Marc got up and closed the door behind them. He stood there, folded his arms, and smiled as he took in the moment.

He nodded to himself and then said out loud, "You know, Phil just may be right. I might be just as good a doctor as him."

# Chapter 26

It wasn't typical that Phil saw his patients outside of the office. Mariah was a special circumstance. Matthew Sallinger, on the other hand, well, he could be considered special too. He was wheelchair bound. He told Phil that he was always just sitting at home in that chair, so he preferred to, and actually opened up more, when he was out strolling. They met weekly at the park across the street from his home. Phil welcomed the break from his office and the breath of fresh air, so he had no problem fulfilling Mr. Sallinger's request.

"Truthfully," Mr. Sallinger said as he and Phil followed the sidewalk in the local park. "This has had no bearing on my professional life at all." He tapped the wheel of his chair. "I've been working sixty to seventy hours a week. If anything, I am much more focused and more productive now."

"Why do you think that is?" Phil asked.

"The accident didn't affect my mental capacity or my ability to think. Plus, I was angry afterward, and I think I just poured it all into my work."

"It didn't affect your ability to feel, did it?"

"No. I just haven't been ready to try the dating thing again, all things considered. I don't do rejection real well."

"I know you don't want pity . . . and I don't pity you," Phil said as he thought about how strong Mr. Sallinger had to be. A drunk driver had hit him head on, and his back was broken in the crash. He was now paralyzed from the waist down.

"If anything, I envy you the strength it took for you to overcome your circumstance. I'd like to think I would be strong enough to handle your situation, but honestly, I don't know. Sometimes I catch myself complaining about little aches and pains. Then I think about what you go through on a daily basis, and I quickly stop whining. You are an extremely strong-willed person, Mr. Sallinger, and you have to live your personal life with that same strength."

"Sounds real good, Doc, but you and I both know that it's not easy in this day and age, trying to find somebody that will see me for me."

"You're right. It's going to be hard, and it's going to take some time. There are still some good women out there, but you have to put forth some effort. If you keep hiding behind your work, you might miss out on somebody amazing. You gotta get back in the game. You know?"

Hold up. Was Phil quoting the same advice Marc had given to him?

Mr. Sallinger shrugged. "Yeah, it's about that time."

"Look," Phil said, motioning to the cityscape in front of them. "There's love out there somewhere for you, brother."

As Mr. Sallinger and Phil continued moving forward, the words Phil had just spoken to his patient replayed in his head.

*There are still some good women out there, but you have to put forth some effort. If you keep hiding behind your work, you might miss out on somebody amazing. You gotta get back in the game. You know?*

*Yeah, I know,* Phil said to himself. He then looked to his patient.

"Mr. Sallinger, I know we still have a few minutes, but I just thought of something I really need to do. If I don't do it now, I—"

Mr. Sallinger shooed Phil away. "Go right ahead. I'm going to hang out here a little bit longer. I'll see you next time."

Phil gave him a slap on the back. "Thank you, Mr. Sallinger. I will see you soon," he said as he headed back to the office.

When Phil entered the lobby, Julie was at her desk. She hadn't said two words to Phil all day. She wasn't giving him the cold shoulder or anything, but she wasn't going out of her way to talk to him either.

"Are you going to be free this evening?" Phil asked her.

She looked up at him strangely. She knew this man was not about to act like he hadn't practically stamped a booty call label on her forehead. Still, she knew she had to take some of the blame. When they started their little rendezvous, she had agreed that she could handle a no-strings-attached relationship with Phil, but she had no idea her heart wouldn't line up with her head. That wasn't Phil's fault, so ignoring him and completely pushing him away wasn't fair to him. Besides, there were women out there playing the same game as men. Why should she be any different? She didn't like it, but perhaps she could get used to it. After all, Phil made her feel like no man had ever made her feel before when making love to her. Why should she deprive herself of that?

"Yeah, I'm free," Julie said dryly.

Phil was a little surprised that Julie had said yes so quickly. He was almost certain she would have made him squirm a little after how upset she was the other day.

"Can you swing by my place about eight?" Phil asked her.

"I guess." She didn't want to seem overly excited. "What's this about?"

"Just need to talk to you, and not here in the office," Phil said. "Can you be there at eight?"

"I'll be there at eight."

Later on that evening, Julie was in Phil's living room, on the couch. Phil was sitting down, trying to look busy arranging magazines on the coffee table. He was trying to do anything to keep from saying what he had to say. Earlier, after talking with Mr. Sallinger, he'd been so sure and confident, but now, not so much.

"Why do I get the feeling that you're stalling?" Julie asked Phil.

"I'm not stalling," he replied. "There are just a couple things that need to be resolved tonight." There was a knock at the door. "One second, please," Phil said as he got up to answer it. He opened the door and then said, "Come on in," as if he had been expecting another guest. Maybe he was, but Julie sure wasn't.

"Maybe I should leave," Julie said, getting up from the couch once she saw Denise enter, dressed to the nines.

"No, stay," Phil said to Julie, holding out his hand to stop her from leaving.

"No, I think I—"

"Julie, stay. Please," Phil said.

Denise stood there a little confused, but she wasn't about to let any intimidation by Julie's presence show on her face. It was glaringly obvious that something big was about to happen.

Julie sat down. "Hi, Denise. It's good to see you," she said, trying not to show how awkward she felt but failing miserably.

"Julie." Denise nodded and smiled as she remained standing.

Phil looked to Denise. "I called you here because when you came to see me, you asked me some questions that I didn't have the answer for. I need to answer those questions, not so much for you, but for me." Phil paused for a second, took a breath, and began. "Yes, I still think about you sometimes. We were together for almost four years, so how could I not? You asked me if I still loved you."

Julie braced herself for the answer to that question. She knew she may not want to hear it.

"I always loved you very much."

Hearing Phil say those words put a smile on Denise's face and a lump in Julie's throat.

Phil paused again, making both women anxious.

"But I don't anymore," Phil said to Denise, wiping that victory smile right off her face. "I'm a good man, and I deserve a good woman—which is why Julie is here."

Julie's eyes lit up.

"But I . . . I don't understand," Denise said. "Then why am I here?"

Little did Phil know that underneath the coat, Denise was wearing a piece of lingerie that he'd always enjoyed seeing her in. When Phil had called her and invited her over, she was certain that he'd come to his senses and was going to stop playing games so they could get back together. If he wanted to still be engaged, she'd even be engaged. She had a girlfriend who had been engaged for almost three years, so she had no doubt she could prolong an engagement with Phil to suit her purposes.

"You're here because I need you to know that it's really over," Phil said. He looked to Julie. "And I needed Julie to know that you know. Communication is key in every relationship." He turned back to Denise. "So have I communicated things clearly? There is no need for you to drop by the office, my home, or anywhere else I might be. And no need to call either."

Denise opened her mouth to say something, but what could she say? The man had made himself very clear. She looked to Julie, giving her the stank face.

· "I'm a good communicator too," Julie said. "So I hope you understand when I say that I need you to get the hell out of my man's house."

Phil cut his eyes in pleasant surprise at Julie. He had never seen this kind of fire in her, and he liked it. Her tone—and her referring to Phil as her man—had turned him on.

Denise raised her hands in surrender at Julie, shook her head, and then began to back pedal to the door.

"One more thing," Phil said to Denise. "I was going to keep the ring, but why? Here." Phil pulled the cherry-wood box from his pocket and handed it to her. "I do wish you the best, and I hope you end up happy."

Denise stared down at the box. "Just a few months ago this ring meant something." She looked at Phil. "You sure about this? 'Cause if I walk out this door—"

"I'm sure," Phil said.

Denise looked down at the box again. "You know what? I will take the ring. I'll keep it in a safe place, just in case we ever need it again." She gave Julie a mischievous look and then walked out the door.

Phil looked at Julie, who sat there quietly at first.

"Now what?" Phil said.

A huge smile covered Julie's face. "Now this!" she said and then jumped up, ran over to Phil, and kissed him.

"So this is . . . this thing between me and you . . .?" She pointed to herself and then pointed to Phil.

"Official," Phil confirmed. "This is official. We are a couple."

They kissed again, and then Julie pulled back. "I am so happy about all this, but I have a question. Why the hell would you give her that ring back?"

"I ain't stupid. That box is empty. I took that ring back and got a couple watches, and I still have some store credit left over." Phil laughed. "I also got these." Phil pulled out two airline tickets from his pocket.

"What is this?" Julie asked.

"Plane tickets for our vacation. I just booked them today."

"What?" Julie exclaimed.

"Seven days and six nights in the Bahamas."

"Are you serious?" Julie snatched the tickets out of Phil's hand.

"Yes."

"But who's going to watch the office?"

"Marc can handle it. I trust him."

Julie raised an eyebrow.

"Seriously. The office will be okay." He kissed Julie then pulled back and looked her in the eyes.

Julie started undressing as she walked toward the bedroom.

"What are you doing?" Phil asked her while enjoying the little strip tease.

"I'm gonna start thanking you for this right now." She patted the airline tickets. "Come on. And on your way to the bedroom, grab the whipped cream and a Red Bull."

"A Red Bull?" Phil questioned. "No red wine?"

"Nope." Julie licked her lips. "A Red Bull, because you're gonna need the energy."

Phil took off his shirt as he ran to the fridge. Wanting to give her a surprise, Phil stripped completely naked in the kitchen, grabbed a Red Bull, cracked it open, and drank some. Then he opened the whipped cream and headed to the bedroom.

"Look at you," Julie said. She was lying in bed, already butt naked.

Phil just stood there for a moment, admiring this magnificent specimen of a woman who in his California king bed. She was his woman, and he liked that idea very much. He was completely open to finding out just how great their love affair could be, but for now, for tonight, he knew exactly what was on the menu. Julie.

"You look . . . tasty."

"It tastes better than it looks," Julie said with a smirk. "And after all, it is yours."

"I like the sound of that, and you are absolutely right. I'm yours, and you're mine."

"You my man, huh?" Julie asked.

"You know it," Phil said, leaning down to kiss her on the lips. "And you are my lady."

Julie pushed Phil away angrily. "Your lady?" She went from zero to a hundred in attitude.

Confused, Phil said, "Yes. Did I say something wrong?"

Julie pointed to the window. "Yeah, out there in the streets I'm a lady, but right now"—she leaned back on the pillows and spread her legs wide—"in these here sheets, I'm your freak." She ran her tongue over her top teeth.

A mischievous smile covered Phil's face as he slowly made his way onto the bed, letting the anticipation build. He knew from the times they had made love before that she was probably already very wet. She had the sweetest little ocean down there. Phil set the whipped cream canister on the bed, drank the rest of the Red Bull, tossed the can over his shoulder, and straddled Julie.

Phil slowly picked out several places on Julie, other than the obvious ones, to apply some whip cream. He then kissed it all off, driving Julie crazy in the best possible way. Then Phil graduated to the most prized and treasured areas of her body and gave them the thousand kisses they deserved. He continued this most intimate conversation with her body until he gave Julie an electric, out of body experience. He loved that he knew how to make her cum in many different ways. It also meant that she was present and connected to him and that she trusted him.

Phil couldn't wait any more. He grabbed both of her ankles and pulled her to him, startling her pleasantly. Her surprise turned into bliss as Phil took her like she was supposed to be taken. One moment he made love to her like he missed her and might never see her again; the next, he was fucking her like he was mad at her. All the while, Julie loved it, needed it, and kissed him like she never wanted to be without him and the way he so masterfully played her body like a musical instrument.

After the loving was done, Phil lay on Julie's chest. He listened to her breathing and to her heartbeat, occasionally kissing her stomach as she rubbed his head.

"You got baby-daddy hair," Julie said, and they both fell out laughing.

"Woman, you are something else," Phil said to Julie.

"Me? So are you! I feel like getting up, heading to the mall, and using up that store credit to get you a wedding band and propose to you," she said playfully.

There was dead silence in the room

Julie turned to Phil. "Too soon?" she asked.

"Too soon," Phil replied as he laughed and shook his head. "But I know what it's not too soon for: another round of good lovin'." Phil turned to Julie and kissed her deeply, and part two of the lovefest had begun.

Maybe bringing up the whole marriage thing was a little soon for Phil, but he knew that somewhere in the near future, it would be a definite possibility. For now, Phil was in love and in lust with the most amazing woman that he had ever met, other than his mom. Life was good, work was abundant, his mother and father were getting along great, Marc had matured and begun realizing his potential, and Mariah was doing better and had even met a guy. The world wasn't perfect, but it was pretty damn close for now.

*Not bad, Dr. Feelgood. Not bad at all*, he thought with a satisfied smile.